FOREWORD

We were both born and raised in Salem and are both interested in history, especially that of our native city. For better or worse, Salem, although its history is rich and diverse, is best known for the awful events associated with the witchcraft hysteria of 1692. A fascination with those events draws large numbers of tourists to Salem every year.

The span of more than 300 years clouds much about Salem's witchcraft tragedy in mystery, from its actual cause, which has been widely speculated upon and written about, to all manner of minutiae. For example, the precise location of Gallows Hill, generally accepted as the place of execution, is a matter of conjecture.

One of the more interesting puzzles about what happened in Salem in 1692 concerns the fate of the remains of the nineteen people, fourteen women and five men, who were hanged for witchcraft. Family tradition has it that Rebecca Nurse's sons recovered her body after her execution and buried her on her property. A skeleton believed to be that of George Jacobs was unearthed on his farmstead many years after his execution and reburied with an appropriate ceremony at the Rebecca Nurse Homestead in 1992.

The whereabouts of the remaining seventeen victims is unknown. That mystery is the focus of this story. *Salem's Secret* is a work of fiction with threads of historical fact running through it. For instance, George Burroughs' successful recitation of prayer before his execution as a test of his innocence and Cotton Mather's statements and actions at that event are based on fact. The conversation between Jonathan Corwin and Cotton Mather the evening of the execution is not.

Philip English, a wealthy merchant, was, along with his wife, accused of witchcraft in 1692. The couple successfully fled Salem and returned when the hysteria was over. The ordeal, however, seriously affected English's finances and the health of his wife. More important, English's anti-puritan feelings most certainly were intensified and he did found an Anglican church in Salem. His role in this story, however, is open to speculation.

Finally, we might add, Stone Harbor doesn't exist and none of the characters in the contemporary portion of this book have real-life counterparts.

R.E.C. and W.L.S. Salem, Massachusetts

Prologue

Salem, Massachusetts August 19, 1692

As the Reverend George Burroughs recited the Lord's Prayer, the gathering looked up at him with rapt attention and expectation. Although he was a short man, Burroughs was powerfully built and was, altogether, a commanding presence.

Some of those gathered had come from inland. They were farmers and farmers' wives and children, mainly. Some of them were accustomed to looking up at George Burroughs and listening to him pray or preach, although they had last done that ten years ago when he had been minister, not of the mother church here in Salem Town, but at the Salem Village Meetinghouse just a few miles from the coast.

"Thy kingdom come, Thy will be done," Burroughs was saying, his gaze fixed heavenward. His voice was strong and clear. Indeed, he was renowned as a man of exceptional strength and now his voice seemed to reflect that quality as well as a strength of some great purpose.

It wasn't just the difference of ten years that distinguished this recital of the prayer by Burroughs from his previous recitals. An additional difference was that rather than sitting on the stern wooden seats of the meetinghouse, those listening to George Burroughs were standing outside, atop a hill in summer sunshine.

Another difference was that rather than standing alone at a pulpit, Burroughs stood on high with three other men and one woman.

But the strangest and most obvious difference was that rather than his clerical garb, the Reverend George Burroughs wore a noose around his neck. And so, too, did the three other men and the woman wear nooses around their necks.

"And forgive us our debts as we forgive our debtors," Burroughs said even as his mind went back to that day in March when he had been brought down to Salem from his home in Wells, Maine.

It had been the girls, young Ann Putnam and Abigail Williams who had cried out against him. His physical strength and the misfortune of two wives dying had been used as evidence of his consorting with Satan.

But he was innocent and he was proving it now with his strong, clear voice and his flawless recitation of the dear Lord's own prayer.

His rendition appeared to be quite moving, for some of those watching him and listening to him had been inspired to tears. Their crying mingled with bird song and soughing wind.

"Amen," Burroughs concluded.

There. It was done. The test of innocence had been passed.

The Reverend George Burroughs looked about him, down at the throng looking back up at him, some of them still crying, some, though, scarcely able to restrain their anticipation.

He looked at those others who had been condemned standing with him and smiled. John Procter had at last composed himself and waited stoically. He had, shortly before, declared himself not yet ready to die and had requested more time. His pleas were refused.

Old George Jacobs held himself as erect as his crippled body would allow and peered out with the dignity afforded by age and knowledge of his own innocence.

John Willard stood steady as the tree from whose limb they would all soon swing. His situation was peculiar. A former deputy constable, he had arrested some of those first accused until he turned on the accusers and renounced the madness. He was cried out against and accused of committing several murders as a witch. As was usual, the accusations were tantamount to proof of guilt.

And Martha Carrier, all the way from Andover and the sole woman at the gallows this time, stood quiet and resigned. The girls from Salem Village had accused her of being the Queen of Witches. To Burroughs, she looked frail and ordinary. But, after all, he had been accused of being King.

Now the tears and murmurings grew stronger and the throng surged as if to prevent the hangman from performing his duty. The prayer had been heard and God's will it seemed would be done by these good people assembled upon Gallows Hill.

"Look," a girl's voice cried suddenly, cutting through the voices and sobs. "The black man is at his shoulder and speaks to him. See him. He whispers in the minister's ear."

The throng stilled, its collective indecision giving it pause. Eyes probed the air around the Reverend George Burroughs' shoulders for a sign of the Dark One.

"No, no," a man's voice said. "The Devil cannot recite the Lord's Prayer."

As if one voice, an assent to this declaration welled from the throng.

"Satan cannot pray for the minister," another man's voice said. The sentiment seemed to be gathering momentum. It appeared that the good people gathered at Gallows Hill would force the release of George Burroughs.

Suddenly, a man astride a white horse forced his mount between the throng and the platform on which the condemned stood.

Pointing up at George Burroughs, Cotton Mather said, "He was never ordained. He is not a minister of God."

The people stood still and hushed. A gull, which had been inspecting the flank of the North River, banked overhead, mewed a series of notes, and headed back toward the river.

The people looked from George Burroughs to Cotton Mather astride his horse. They looked at one another and grappled with indecision. Mather was well known to most of them. Despite his youth—he was not yet 30—he was himself a commanding presence, dressed in black and standing in his stirrups atop the white mount.

"Besides," Mather said, his voice pitched so that the good people had to be silent to hear him. "Besides," he repeated, "the Devil often transforms himself into an angel of light."

For a moment, as this statement worked into the collective consciousness of the throng, all was quiet save for the wind and the distant screech of a jay.

Mather's horse grew restive, clacking its hooves and whinnying. Mather quieted the animal, turned his gaze to the hangman, and nodded.

The throng, now without resolve, watched as George Burroughs was slung over the hangman's burly shoulder and carried up the ladder.

For a moment, the noose and rope hung slack until the hangman made the drop.

Magistrate Jonathan Corwin and his guest, Cotton Mather, sat in Corwin's comfortable home less than a mile distant from Gallows Hill where earlier that day George Burroughs and the four other condemned witches had been hanged. Dusk had been snuffed and the two men drank wine by candle in the warm air of the August evening.

They looked out to the road that led from the gaol to Gallows Hill, the road the condemned had traveled earlier, chained in an oxcart.

"The man was the Devil incarnate. I know it," Mather was saying. "The Devil whispers in his ear. Indeed. He is the Devil."

Jonathan Corwin mumbled something, neither assent nor dissent. This witch business was wearing on him. Five hanged today. Five a month ago. The hangings had started in June with that tavern wench Bridget Bishop. Who knew how many were in jail and yet the accusations still went on. Witches, it seemed, were everywhere.

Corwin looked about him. Some of the wretches had been examined here in his very home. He shuddered as he thought of the stink of them.

He sipped some wine and thought of today's hangings. Burroughs' recitation of the Lord's Prayer had been perfect. He wondered about that. And at his pretrial examination back in March, the man's body had been free of any witch's marks. He had been marvelously muscled, though. It was no wonder he had had such strength.

"I want his head," Mather said abruptly.

Corwin stared for a moment. "What did you say?" he said finally.

"I want George Burroughs' head. I want to study it."

Corwin poured himself more wine and then remembered to offer the bottle to Mather.

Making a motion of dismissal with his hand, Mather said, "You can help me. I want to go to the grave. To Gallows Hill. You know people."

Corwin knew what Mather meant. George Corwin, his nephew, was the High Sheriff of Essex County and would, if his uncle requested it, not interfere with body tampering.

"They're denied Christian burial," he said softly.

"Rightfully so. They are themselves a desecration. They have forsaken their Lord and God. They will never have a proper burial in consecrated ground."

Neither man spoke of what they both knew. That already one witch had been removed from the fissure in the earth beside Gallows Hill that served as a common grave. Rebecca Nurse had been presumably taken back to her farm by her *sons and buried somewhere on that property.*

In his mind's eye, Corwin saw Burroughs' body thrown into the fissure that day. His shirt and trousers had been removed.

Corwin tried to blink away what else he had seen. Burroughs' chin and one of his hands had remained uncovered when the dirt had been thrown over him. At least he wouldn't be hard to find.

"Will you help me?" Mather asked.

Someone rode by and in the gathering moonlight Corwin saw little clouds of dust raised by the horse's hooves.

He took another sip of wine and looked at Cotton Mather. "My nephew will see to it that no one will interfere with you."

(Salem, Massachusetts over 300 years later)

He sat in the car and watched the house. The mid-July evening was sultry and thick with sullen, black clouds that grumbled, complained and threatened to spill. The thunder was building and made an interesting complement to the somber classical music playing from the car's radio. Bach. *O Haupt voll Blut und Wunden.* The blend suited him.

The house was a First Period, which meant it was very old even by the standards of this city where many houses dated back to before the American Revolution. It had a high, peaked roof with several gables and a massive chimney. It was stained a deep brown and the clapboards were fastened with old, rustic-looking nails. The casement windows with their small diamond panes were swung open.

Lightning etched a jagged scar through the black sky and its crack made the man jump a bit in his seat. It was close. The wind gusted and tousled the trees. A few drops speckled his windshield.

On the second floor of the house, he saw the woman at a window, cranking it in. That's where she lived: on the second floor. The bottom floor was the shop—or shoppe, as she touted it, a too obvious affectation for his money—where she sold her pagan trinkets and apparently made quite a decent living doing so.

No. *Decent* wasn't the word. Not at all. As far as the man was concerned, it was a very *indecent* living and it just went to prove what gullible fools the people were who had anything at all to do with the woman, who bought anything from her.

But that would change very soon if things went as planned. He thought of the Bible, a book he knew very well indeed. *Thou shalt not suffer a witch to live.* Exodus. He said the words to himself and smiled.

Now she was at another upstairs window, cranking it in. He thought of his house. He could trust Emma Wilt to be shutting the windows against the rain. Reliable Emma. A bit of a snoop but very reliable.

The woman had to lean out a bit to crank the window, affording him a very good glimpse of her ample and, for his money, quite attractive figure. He'd give her that. She was quite attractive. Aristocratic face and bountiful figure, just the way he liked it. Not for him those twigs that you saw in magazines promoting lipstick and the latest fashions from Paris.

But he wasn't here in any kind of pathetic Peeping Tom capacity. This was just a simple reconnaissance, a tactic driven more by curiosity than necessity.

It really was a shame he had to do what he had to do. Well, he wouldn't actually do anything himself. He had others who would tend to the actual—His mind fumbled for a word. Work. The actual work.

A bolt and a boom banged the sky and the wind picked up some more, almost alarmingly. Then the rain fell in cascades. The man started his engine, rolled up his windows, and put the air conditioner on full blast. The wipers, at high speed, lost their battle with the rain and he couldn't see the woman anymore. No matter. Operations would soon begin.

He put the car in drive and prepared to pull away. Despite the air conditioner, the inside of the car was warm and humid and he ran a finger under his clerical collar as he thought again of the passage from Exodus.

Rebecca Nurse Homestead

George Jacobs Farm House

Chapter One

Helen Waters brought her forty footer to the edge of the float and cut the engine. She was aware of the stares of the other fishermen and a handful of tourists as they looked down at her. The stares didn't bother her even though she knew most of the fishermen wanted her to screw up, maybe bang up her boat or the float. They resented a woman wrestling a living from the sea.

She knew there was something else in their stares too. She was aware of their eyes probing beneath the baggy shirt and the baggy jeans tucked into high fisherman's boots. The loose, unglamorous clothing couldn't hide the woman doing the difficult and dangerous work that for generations had been done by only the strongest and bravest of men.

From its mid-morning angle, the late August sun glinted off the water and Helen's copper hair pinned up off her neck. She looked up at Charlie Goodwin, her wholesaler, and smiled. At least Charlie didn't want her to screw up.

Helen reached into the hold of the *Working Girl* and pulled out a net squirming and wriggling like some kind of sea creature in its death throes. She lifted the net over a hogshead and spilled her catch of lobsters into it. Some of the tourists made little noises of approval as they caught sight of the green-black creatures tumbling from the net into the barrel.

Capping the barrel, Helen turned it on its side and rolled it to the ramp slanting up from the side of the *Working Girl* to the top of the pier.

She paused a moment and then rolled it up to Charlie Goodwin as the tourists murmured delight at her strength and skill and the fishermen looked down with menacing eyes.

Lincoln Southwick adjusted the filter mask over his mouth and nose and prepared to pull out part of the crumbling fieldstone foundation to the Stone Harbor Episcopalian church.

On the whole, the foundation was in amazingly good condition considering the church sat just across the street from the ocean and over the years had been punched and kicked by who knew how many nor'easters and a handful of hurricanes in Lincoln's lifetime alone. The church had been built in 1701, Lincoln knew, long before careful weather records were kept.

He probed at some crumbling mortar with his mason's hammer for a few minutes before he had to wipe the beads of sweat from his forehead. He was sitting in the sun on the grass in front of the church which blocked the land breeze. He lowered the mask, took a pull from his water bottle, and sat back to watch the activity at Fisherman's Pier and wish he were there laughing and joking and slapping backs with the guys.

Why the hell had he let that damned minister talk him into doing a little freebie work on the damned crumbling foundation of the church?

He knew why. Helluva thing for a minister to have something on you.

He could see that a boat had just pulled up. He squinted against the sun and shaded his eyes. It was the *Working Girl*.

Now he really wished he were at the pier. In his book, Helen Waters was worth watching anytime, doing anything. Even when she was wearing her fishing clothes.

He smiled as he thought of her. Spunky gal, she was, taking over her Dad's business the way she had after the sea had taken him. He knew that most everyone in Stone Harbor had bet she'd never last. But it was going on two years and she showed every sign of lasting and even thriving.

He pulled the mask back down and turned to the wall, the mask covering the smile as he thought of her.

At the top of the pier, Helen righted the hogshead and looked up at a grinning Charlie Goodwin. Charlie was shaking his head slowly with admiration.

"Dammit, Helen, you're something else. I'm still amazed every time I see you roll one of those hogsheads up the ramp. No one does that anymore."

"Dad did. He said, you want an easy life, you won't be a fisherman. You want easy work, be a lumberjack or lion tamer."

Helen rested her hand on the mechanized ramp that everyone used nowadays to bring their catch up from the boat to the pier. "Dad always said, the day I have to use this thing is the day I know I'm not fit to go to sea."

She paused a moment then she smiled again and said, "He showed me how to roll a hogshead and so I do it. Besides, it keeps me in shape."

"Keeps you a goddamn show-off."

Helen recognized the voice but ignored it. It came from the group of fishermen who had watched her arrive and it belonged to Lucien Thibodeau.

"Let's settle up, Charlie," she said.

"Let's settle up, Charlie," Lucien's voice mimicked. The voice was close behind her now. Charlie's head was lowered. He was on Helen's side but he was old and he wanted no trouble.

Helen felt her neck burn. It was from more than the sun. Charlie was fumbling with the top of the hogshead with gnarled fingers. She reached down to help.

"See, there you go. He can do it, for chrissakes."

Helen turned to face Lucien. "I'm just trying to help." She was flustered and hoped it didn't show in her voice. And she was angry for being flustered and for explaining anything to this troglodyte.

As she confronted Lucien, the sun was in her face and she had to squint. At five foot nine, she had almost an inch on him but she was aware of the knots of muscles on his swarthy arms, the deep chest and the thick neck and broad shoulders.

"You know what you're doing, don't you? You're taking a living from some poor slob trying to support a family. It's not like the old days. Fishing, lobstering's bad nowadays. Not enough to go around. And pretty soon the government's gonna really crack down and say, no more. At least for a while."

They were standing close and Helen smelled the hint of booze on his breath.

She couldn't tell whether it was fresh or from last night. Maybe both.

Lucien waved his arm toward the street and its row of stores and shops. "Why don't you open one of those little stores that sell perfumey candles and things like that?"

"Maybe I'll open one that sells mouthwash and sell some to you. You sure could use it."

The mean look in his eyes became meaner and he put a big hand on her shoulder and squeezed. "You little—"

She tried to pull away but the hand was like a clamp.

Behind Lucien, the little cluster of fishermen pulled closer. The sunlight dappled their faces, their expressions mixed. Some seemed embarrassed. Some grinned in amusement.

Lincoln Southwick pulled one of the fieldstones free and set it on the grass. With a little luck, he might get away with re-mortaring about a dozen of the stones on this part of the foundation.

He pulled up the mask, took another pull from the water bottle and stared at the wall. Something wasn't right and it took him a couple of seconds to figure what it was.

He peered into the small hole left by the pulled stone. He saw nothing but black space that stretched beyond the oblique sunlight.

He was familiar with the church's basement. There should be paneling backing up to the foundation. He reached in as far as he could and felt nothing.

Air eddied from the hole. It was sluggish and smelled of time, of dirt, and darkness. Lincoln flared his nostrils and decided he'd put the mask back on before sticking his head inside.

He'd pull another stone and then go to his truck for the flashlight to get a better look.

"Let go of her, Lucien," Charlie Goodwin said. "What's wrong with you?"

"Mind your own business, Charlie. Count the lobsters and butt out," Lucien Thibodeau said.

Helen tried to wrap her hand around Lucien's wrist but the wrist was too thick. Almost as thick as his head, she thought.

"Would you mind taking your hand off my shoulder," she said. "You're acting like an ass."

"Like a what?"

"Like an ass. I could add a syllable but I'm a lady."

They held a brief staring contest, and then Lucien removed his hand. "Sure, if it makes you feel better, I'll let go. I wouldn't want to hurt a lady."

Then quickly his hand shot out, clasped her by the neck, and pulled her close. "How 'bout a kiss?"

He pinned his mouth on hers.

"Go Lucien," one of his friends yelled.

Helen tried to pull free. His breath was disgusting.

Finally, he withdrew his mouth but held onto her neck. Leering, he said, "Now, what did you call me?"

Helen recalled the many lessons her father had taught her, the lessons he would have taught the son he never had. Things like rolling a hogshead up a plank. Like defending herself. But it wasn't just the lessons from her father that now came to the fore. Before taking to the sea, she had spent three years as a police officer in nearby Salem and the situation she was now in was pretty basic.

She jammed her boot down hard on his sneakered foot and, as his hand let go of her neck and he blinked in surprise and pain, she wrapped her left leg behind him and pushed with all her strength on his chest.

She watched him roll a third of the way down the ramp and then fall under the railing and land on his back in the water.

Lucien's friends moaned in protest and the tourists cheered. Some gathered around her and clapped her on the shoulder.

Charlie Goodwin came over to her and said, "Good for you, Helen. He needed that."

He paused and grinned and then slapped his knee theatrically. "You know what I was thinking? I was thinking, come hell and high water, this kid can take care of herself. Honest to God. I wasn't even thinking of the pun on your name. Fits you perfectly, though. Helen Highwater. Bet that's what old Lucien will think of you as from now on."

They looked down the ramp at the sodden, sulking figure who was climbing his way back up to the pier. When he reached the top, he kept his head low and avoided everyone's eyes as he slunk to his pickup truck.

Lincoln Southwick had removed another stone and was about to stick his flashlight and head into the hole when he heard a roar down by the pier.

He looked over and saw a cluster of people looking over the side, some fishermen, the usual tourists, and—unmistakable—the flashing red hair of Helen Waters.

Someone must have gone over. He started to get up but as he watched he could see there was no sense of urgency at the pier. It was more as though something amusing had happened.

He watched for a few minutes until someone came up the ramp.

He shaded his eyes and squinted. Looked like that jerk Lucien Thibodeau. He looked wet and like some kid who's just been birched by the principal.

Lincoln laughed. The jerk must have fallen over.

He'd take a peek inside the hole here and then maybe mosey down to the pier and see what had happened. Maybe get a chance to talk with Helen Waters for a bit.

He adjusted the mask over his mouth and nose to make sure it was snug and stuck his head and flashlight inside.

The beam probed from side to side and then down.

And then froze.

Jesus.

Lincoln stared and started to count.

He got to a dozen and stopped.

He pulled his head back out and stuck the two stones back in place. His heart was ticking pretty hard as he wondered who to tell what he had just seen.

The police, for sure. But they'd be just starters.

One thing was certain. He'd forgotten all about going down to the pier to see what had happened there.

Chapter Two

There were seventeen.

Lincoln Southwick and Dr. Jan Reuter, minister of the church, knelt, cramped, on the stone floor between the outer foundation and the inner one in a hidden room that tapered off one corner of the foundation, ran out to its widest point of about five feet and tapered back in about fifteen feet from the corner.

They were eyeball to eyesocket with seventeen human skeletons.

Lincoln hadn't gone to the police right away. Instead, he called Dr. Reuter who stuck his head in from outside when Lincoln removed a stone for him.

Dr. Reuter then immediately dragged Lincoln into the basement. "Linc," he had said, "we can't go in from the street. We'll have the whole town gawking in. Take down a piece of paneling."

He added 'please' when Lincoln stared coldly.

"There's foundation behind the paneling and it's probably in better shape than the one outside."

"Please."

"Don't you think we should call the cops?"

"Let's see what we have first. Whoever they are, it looks as though they've been there a long, long time."

And so six stones removed and a couple of hours later with Lincoln sweating heavily and wishing he'd obeyed his first impulse and gone to the police, they wedged their way in through the hole he had made.

The skeletons were in two rows, each row two skeletons long, piled four deep except one that had five.

They had been laid to rest neatly.

There was no decayed gore or remnants of clothing. Although the ambiance wasn't pleasant, there was no death smell.

"Look at that one," Jan Reuter said, pointing to the row five skeletons deep. "Second one from the top."

Lincoln Southwick squinted. "I don't—"

"No skull," Reuter said.

"Jesus."

"Please," the minister said.

"Sorry."

They stared for a moment.

"He was a small one," Lincoln said. "I mean, even if you throw in a head, he was short."

"Might have been a woman."

Lincoln shook his head. "Maybe. I'm no expert but that looks like the skeleton of someone who was pretty rugged."

He started to reach for the bones.

"Don't touch," Reuter said sharply.

Lincoln Southwick took a deep breath and said, "I don't know about you, but I've seen all I want to. I say we call the cops."

Jan Reuter looked sad when he stood next to Lincoln back outside the hole. They brushed their knees. "When word of this gets out, we'll have a mob here. It'll be like a carnival."

"I suspect so," Lincoln said. He wondered whether the minister was hinting that he mortar the stones back in and they agree to not saying anything to anyone.

"Linc, I'd appreciate your keeping this to yourself. I mean until I can get Erle Symmes over here to see what's what. I suppose he'll have to get all kinds of state people in on this."

Lincoln nodded. Erle Symmes was Stone Harbor's police chief.

"I won't say anything," he said as he looked at the minister closely, "but you better call him right away. I mean, that's a lotta skeletons in your closet, Jan."

Lincoln knew the minister didn't like him to call him Jan and that he dreaded anything that would reflect negatively on the church. He enjoyed watching him squirm a little.

It was pleasant to turn the tables and have something on him for a change.

Mabel Waters was reading by the window in a shaft of late afternoon sunlight when her granddaughter squeezed her 1986 Chevy pickup into the driveway, the tires crunching on the small stones. In this, the old part of Stone Harbor, driveways weren't spacious or curving and backing the truck in from the street took as much dexterity as mooring a boat or threading a needle.

The truck had to be backed in because backing out onto a street not much wider than the driveway itself where drivers seemed to think they were on a four-lane was attempted only by the suicidal.

Helen Waters kissed her grandmother on the forehead. "What are you reading?"

"Trash. Supposed to be a mystery. I'm on page fifty and I've got it figured out already."

"Are you sure? Maybe the writer wants you to think you've figured it out."

"No. I looked ahead. I was right."

Helen nodded, hid a smile, and didn't ask why her grandmother was still reading the book. Five other books from the Stone Harbor Public Library sat on a table beside her. Helen examined the covers. Two other mysteries, a Western, and two non-fiction, one on the plight of the world's rain forests and a biography of Lyndon Johnson. Mabel Waters' reading tastes were eclectic.

Helen sniffed the air and looked toward the kitchen. "Smells good. What's for supper?" This was her grandmother's week to cook.

"Leftover stew. Monday's chicken, Tuesday's steak tips, and Wednesday's lamb. Throw in some potatoes, carrots, and turnip simmered in olive oil and you have a Mabel Waters original." She wrinkled her nose. "Does smell good, doesn't it? We'll know how it tastes pretty soon."

She put her book down and looked at her granddaughter. She saw herself before her hair turned and the years had bent her back and withered her limbs and stretched her skin. She saw her son, a tall, handsome man she'd never stop crying to herself for. And she saw her daughter-in-law whom she had loved like a daughter. The sea had taken her son and the highway his wife.

Mabel Waters had only this woman left who lived from the sea as generations of Waters had. And Helen had only her grandmother. To be sure, for Helen there had been and there still were men. Mabel knew there were lots of men who'd die to hook Helen Waters but she was too independent and too restless and the sea was too demanding to let her be tied up to shore life. "That'll all come later," Helen always told her grandmother. "Maybe someday if I get a teaching job I'll settle down."

"How was your day?" Mabel Waters asked.

"So-so." Helen thought of what Lucien Thibodeau had said about the government regulating catches and what he had said about her taking a living away from a man. She didn't feel like talking about either and she surely didn't want to tell her grandmother about pushing Thibodeau off the pier.

She smiled. "I want to grab a quick shower before we eat."

"Talked with Jenny Perkins today," Mabel said. Met her at the library. You know Jenny, don't you? Does some housekeeping at the Episcopal Church. Now here's one for you. Seems they were doing some work on the church's foundation, pulling out some of the stones or whatever."

"Who? Jenny?"

Mabel Waters laughed. "No. That Southwick boy. You know, Lincoln Southwick."

"Oh, him."

"Anyway, they ran into quite a little surprise. Had to call in Erle Symmes and then some bigwig from the State Police."

"All right, so tell me. What did they find?"

"Skeletons. Human skeletons. Seventeen of them. Jenny heard them talking."

"The skeletons?"

"Oh, you're just like your father with that sense of humor."

Helen Waters patted her grandmother's head. "It's not at all funny, is it?" She thought of seventeen human skeletons.

"Apparently they had been there a long time, from what Jenny was able to gather."

"Well, that church sure is old."

"One of the skeletons had no skull," Mabel Waters said, savoring the drama of the pronouncement.

"Jan Reuter must be beside himself. That man is so sanctimonious."

"Juicy, isn't it? Well, you take your shower and I'll set the table. Then we'll watch the six o'clock news to see if anything's out on this yet."

Helen Waters was toweling herself and still mulling what her grandmother had told her when a possible significance of seventeen very old human skeletons, one with no skull, hit her.

She sat on the edge of the tub. "Oh, my God," she said aloud.

Chapter Three

The phone, with its memory buttons, had been Helen's idea and Mabel knew why her granddaughter insisted on it. Helen had said, "Oh, it's so much better, Gram. When you call your friends or the library all you do is press the button beside their number."

That's what Helen had said but Mabel Waters knew it was really for the button with 9-1-1 beside it. She knew her granddaughter wanted her to have quick access to the fire and police departments and the ambulance when Helen wasn't home.

When your number's up, it's up, Mabel felt and she hoped when the pain came it would be quick and merciful. She didn't want to be able to crawl to the phone, punch a number, and wait for the whooping ambulance to rescue her for an existence of confinement away from her books, her cooking, and her plants.

Besides, the phone didn't seem right to her. Push a memory button, get a little jingle, get a little tune. She remembered the days when you just picked up the receiver and Lucy Thomas or Sarah McHenry would say, "Number, please." Those days were long gone and so were Lucy and Sarah.

If you had wanted to, you could have a little conversation with Lucy or Sarah before you even got to the party you were calling. But not with this phone. Push the button, listen to the little two-second tune, and be ready to talk.

It was like with that damn microwave that Helen had bought. No question it was quick. A quick path to awful taste.

She sighed as she pushed the button beside Ione Arrington's name. Each time she pushed it, it was as if she were giving in. But Helen had bought her the phone and had programmed the numbers and a couple of times caught Mabel punching the series of numbers instead of just the programmed button.

Ione Arrington, whose mother had been reading *The Last Days of Pompeii* when she was carrying Ione and named her child after a character in the book, answered, her voice light and alert and not sounding at all as if it belonged to an eighty-one year old.

The two friends chatted a few moments about the skeletons discovered in the church basement the previous day, the weather, and books they were reading before Mabel said, "That Monahan boy called this morning."

"Nice boy, nice-looking boy. I always thought he and Helen make a handsome couple."

"Hmmm. Oh, they do and I like Bo Monahan. He's a decent man—"

"But," Ione interrupted.

"What do you mean, 'but'?"

"I sense a 'but,' that's all. You were going to say, 'He's a decent man, but.' Something was coming next and I think I can guess what."

"Think you're so smart, don't you, Ione? All right, tell me. What was I going to say?"

"You were going to say, 'He's a decent man, but he's a fisherman.'"

"Well, he is."

"And a good one. Times are hard now but he's making a good, honest living."

"It's no life."

"I'm surprised at you. Your husband, his father, his grandfather, and your son were all fishermen. Your granddaughter's a fisherman. The sea is a way of life for the Waters and there's nothing to be ashamed of about it."

"It can kill a person, Ione. I want better for Helen than to be a fisherman or a fisherman's wife. I want her to get interested in a nice doctor or lawyer."

"Mabel, she's a grown woman and she has a mind of her own."

"Oh, why do I talk to you? You're no help."

"Don't get huffy. We'll talk some more over lunch. I'll pick you up in an hour and then I have an idea. We'll see someone who may be able to help you."

Helen Waters parked the pick-up truck across from the church and locked it. Its paint was faded and some rust spots were beginning to blossom here and there but mechanically it was sound and she couldn't afford to have it stolen. Even in Stone Harbor where auto theft and other forms of crime were rare you had to use reasonable caution. Besides, she had some loose change on the dashboard and she couldn't afford to lose even that.

After coming in off the *Working Girl* at mid-afternoon, she had showered the ocean and fish smell off her body and changed her clothes. In a casual denim blouse and jeans she knew she wasn't exactly dressed for church but this wasn't Sunday and she wasn't going to service.

She went to the minister's house beside the church and rang the bell.

Jenny Perkins, the housekeeper, answered the door.

"He's busy right now," she said to Helen's request to see Dr. Jan Reuter. "What's it about?"

"It's about what I imagine he's still trying to keep a secret."

Nothing had appeared in the afternoon Stone Harbor *Buoy* about the discovery of the skeletons. So far, only a few people seemed to have heard of what Lincoln Southwick had uncovered but the lid couldn't be kept on too long.

Jenny Perkin's features composed themselves into a guarded look. "You're the Waters girl, aren't you? Why don't I tell Dr. Reuter you were here and I'm sure he'll get back to you."

"No need, Jenny," Dr. Jan Reuter said. He came from a side room into the hall.

"I always have time for John Waters' girl. Your father was a good man, young lady. Would like to have seen him at church more often but I can understand why a fisherman might need his few precious moments of spare time to himself. The sea can be demanding."

Ignoring the 'young lady,' Helen smiled and wondered whether the minister was about to launch an attack on her own church-going habits and whether he was always this pompous.

"Come in," he said, beckoning Helen into the room he had just come from. Two other men looked at Helen as she came in.

"You know Paul Clarke, I believe," the minister said.

Helen nodded at the church deacon, a middle-aged man of wispy hair and serious mien who always looked to Helen like some kind of Hawthorne character who would have been happier living maybe three-hundred years ago, patrolling the church aisles with the prod to keep nodders awake.

"And this is Joe Sennot. Joe's the State Archaeologist. Joe, this is Helen Waters who, I'm afraid, is not a relic of the past but is very future. She's a fisherman or I suppose I should say a fisherwoman or fisherperson."

"'Fisherman' is fine," Helen said. "It was good enough for my father and it's good enough for me."

Joe Sennot stood and extended a hand. He would not have fit Helen's preconceived notion of an archaeologist. She pegged him in his early thirties. He had ruddy cheeks and scrubbed good looks. A trace of baby fat filled out his blue Oxford button-down shirt at the waist and chest. His smile was warm and friendly. Altogether, he conveyed the air of boyish charm and appeal.

Helen liked what she saw. She took his hand and smiled back. She could guess why he was here.

"Now what's all this about a secret?" Jan Reuter asked after he directed Helen to a chair.

"The skeletons. A few tongues are wagging about them and it won't be long before the *Buoy* and the Boston papers pick up on it, I imagine."

"No secret, I assure you. As a matter of fact, that's why Mr. Sennot is here. But why did you want to see me about them?"

Helen looked at the three men and suddenly wondered whether her little theory was foolish. She decided to hold onto it a bit longer, maybe do some more research before divulging it.

"Well, I heard the skeletons appeared to be very old and, as you may know, I'm studying to be a history teacher so I just wondered whether you had any theories about them."

"An interesting combination—fisherman and history teacher." Jan Reuter smiled. "I don't have any theories. But you're right. People will be wondering about the skeletons and we'd like to be able to say something definitive. We hope Mr. Sennot can help us shed some light."

Helen smiled at Joe Sennot. He smiled back.

She then included the others in her smile and stood. "Well, I wish you all luck. It's fascinating, isn't it?"

"I'm just about to leave myself," Joe Sennot said. "I'll walk out with you, Miss Waters."

"Please, it's Helen," she said, as he walked her through the sunshine to her truck.

"Talk about your historical relics," she said, nodding at the truck as she unlocked its door. Instantly, she regretted the comment, feeling it was inane, knowing she had been groping for some bit of small talk.

"You should see what I drive. Actually, I envy you the truck. Sometimes, in my work, I could use one." He extended his hand. "It's been a pleasure meeting you, Helen."

"My pleasure. And I'm looking forward to your finding."

"Might take a while. By the way, could you recommend a restaurant? Thought maybe I'd grab a bite before heading out."

"What do you like?"

He smiled. "If I'm going to eat in Stone Harbor, I suppose anything other than seafood would be treason."

"Do you like lobster?"

"Who doesn't?"

"Boiled lobster?"

"I'm drooling."

"Well, Mr. Sennot," she said, withdrawing her hand and suddenly realizing it had been a long handshake, "how would you like to come to my place and join my grandmother and me. I'll boil us some lobsters that just this morning were roaming the bottom of Stone Harbor as free as could be?"

"I think I'd like that very much and I'd love to meet your grandmother."

"Hop in. I'll drive you to your car."

Loretta Lowell bent her head solemnly over the silk packet of herbs she had concocted. Her hands were spread wide and her eyes were slits. Her lips moved to an arcane incantation.

Mabel Waters and Ione Arrington sat across the table from her in the back room of Loretta's small shop, the Mystic Crypt. Pungent smells of incense and herbs filled the whole store.

As Mabel watched Loretta Lowell, she thought she had never seen such a two-tone person. Her skin looked like a stranger to sunlight. She was as white as a snowman, or snowwoman, in this case, Mabel thought. But her eyes were black, like lumps of coal, to continue the snowwoman analogy. Her hair and eyebrows were also black, so black that Mabel was convinced the color came from a bottle. She wondered about the blackness of the eyes and the whiteness of the skin.

And, of course, her dress or gown or cloak or whatever it was was black.

She looked to Mabel like a human penguin.

But she wasn't a penguin. She was a witch.

An actual witch.

A practitioner of witchcraft. Of Wicca.

They were at the Mystic Crypt at Ione's suggestion. At first, Mabel had been skeptical but Ione was convincing and at the very least the experience of going to a witch for a curse and a love potion would prove interesting,

And, so, here they sat watching Loretta Lowell, one of the many modern-day witches in Salem, a city where witchcraft had been an issue since 1692.

Loretta had already made the curse designed to turn away undesirables, in this case Bo Monahan, from Helen Waters. Now she was working on the love potion which Ione insisted would work because she had a friend whose niece had been the beneficiary of such a charm.

Ione assured her that once she had the potion all that would be left was to wait for a suitable young man for Helen and turn it loose on him.

Loretta had apparently finished her incantation but she kept her head bent over the packet of herbs a moment before looking up. She put the two packets—the curse and the love potion—into a brown paper bag and handed it to Mabel.

"With love and peace," she said.

"Well, one's for love, all right, but the other—I don't know that you could say it's for peace."

"We don't know how things will work out, do we? Maybe in the long run it's for the better if two people don't fall in love or at least one doesn't fall in love with the other."

"How much do I owe you?" Mabel asked.

"Five dollars apiece."

Mabel Waters snapped open her purse, a heavy cloth thing which she had bought when Dwight and Mamie Eisenhower were in the White House.

"Are these guaranteed?"

"Certainly. They are guaranteed to make things happen or not happen as they were meant to."

Mabel sensed smoke and mirrors in the answer but declined to argue. Ten dollars was a small enough price to pay for the chance that she could make things work for her granddaughter. And meeting Loretta Lowell and watching Loretta Lowell had been interesting.

"Lots of people come to Loretta for help. For potions and so on," Ione said.

Loretta Lowell smiled a warm, white-toothed smile that would have been even warmer, Mabel thought, if her lips weren't so dark.

They weren't black exactly but natural or red would definitely have been better. "Indeed they do," she said.

"I can't help feeling it's all so pagan," Mabel said.

"That's exactly what it is," Loretta Lowell said. "But you've got to forget the bad connotations of the word. Pagan simply means non-traditional. It's not Christian, Moslem or Jew. But don't think of it as evil."

"Oh, I don't. I certainly wouldn't be here if I thought that."

"Paganism actually brings us back to our roots. If you go back far enough, all of us had ancestors who were pagan. And it worked for them. Change isn't always for the better."

Loretta Lowell led the two women to the front of the store, through the usual cluster of tourists looking at trinkets and sniffing herbs who were drawn to Salem by a fascination with witches, historical and modern.

As they walked to Ione's car, Mabel thought that if the love potion hooked someone nice for Helen, maybe she'd invite that reclusive old artist Hale Winters over some morning and slip some into his coffee.

He struck quite a picture with his flowing white hair as he sat on the piers doing seascapes. Mabel often thought she and Hale would make a dashing couple.

Chapter Four

She caught him looking away when she had dropped the lobsters into the boiling pot. It was easy to relate to the feeling. As often as she boiled them, she knew she hesitated a millisecond over the bubbling water. The experts said the lobsters didn't feel a thing but no one ever asked a lobster.

"Delicious," Joe Sennot said, as he extracted meat from a claw.

"Traditional," Helen said. "New England classic. It doesn't get much better, does it?"

They had gone through a plate of steamed clams and were attacking their two lobsters each. Corn on the cob, sliced tomatoes and cucumbers, and beer completed the menu. Joe had brought two six packs.

"This would cost a fortune in a restaurant," Joe said.

"Costs me nothing. One of the bennies of being a fisherman. Except that sometimes you get sick of seafood. I really long for a good prime rib every so often."

"That'll be my treat. I'd like to do that real soon, if you'd like."

"Sounds good to me," Helen said, thinking that she and this man she had just met were clicking very fast indeed. "But pizza would be fine too."

"Whatever. We'll decide later."

Their gaze held for a moment.

"So," Helen said, "where are the skeletons now?"

"We removed them. Took all morning and part of the afternoon. We had to be very careful. A lot of tagging. That sort of thing."

"Any theories?"

Joe shrugged and sipped some beer. "I don't like to form theories until I have enough data." He laughed. "God, that sounded stuffy, didn't it? Stuffy and pompous."

"Not at all. Makes sense, actually. So tell me, Joe, how does one get to be State Archaeologist?"

"The title is more impressive than the job but it can be interesting. It is interesting to me. As a kid, I always dreamed of doing digs and so on." Joe laughed. "So as an adult I can now play in the mud in a socially acceptable way. Seriously, though, I loved history and geography so I guess we have something in common. You're studying to be a history teacher, you say."

"Yeah. I love fishing. My dad was a fisherman and took me out often when I was a little girl but it's a tough life and I don't know if I can see myself doing it when I'm middle-aged, let alone old and gray."

"Your dad's not living?"

"No." Helen paused a long moment. "A sudden squall. He was experienced about the ocean but there's always that unknown."

She looked at Joe steadily a moment. "He's still out there."

"Oh, God, I'm sorry."

"It's been a few years but it's still really hard on my grandmother. So," she said quickly, "I'm going for my M.A.T. at the college in Salem and someday I'll be standing in front of a bunch of high school kids trying to breathe life into the past."

"I think fishing would be easier," Joe said with a laugh.

"Where did you go to school, Joe?"

"Yale."

"I'm impressed."

He worked on an ear of corn a moment.

"Here," she said, handing him a napkin. "After lobster, steamers, and corn, you always feel you need a shower."

"I know a fellow who teaches at Salem State College. History department, too. Dermot McKenna. Know him?"

"I've heard the name."

"He and I will talk about Salem hours on end," Joe said. "So much history there but, it's funny, I've never really explored the city."

"I'll be your tour guide some day. I'll show you the sites."

"I want to see where they burned the witches."

"They didn't. They were hanged."

"God, I'm embarrassed. And I told you I loved history."

"It's a common misconception. Nineteen hanged. One man pressed to death. Those poor people. I—Ah, here's my grandmother."

Joe Sennot instantly liked the sprightly old woman. Her gaze and handshake were firm and steady as she appraised him. He noticed her eyes light up at 'State Archaeologist' and 'Yale.'

"Well, well, you two sit down and finish your supper. I'll throw a lobster in the pot and join you, if you don't mind. I'm starved half to death. Spent the afternoon in Salem with Ione doing some shopping. We were going to eat there but I'm glad now we didn't."

"Joe and I were just talking about Salem. Someday maybe I'll show him the witchcraft hysteria sites. I was about to tell him there are lots of modern-day witches in Salem, too."

"That so?" Mabel said. She plunged a wriggling lobster into the pot, scooped some steamed clams from another pot, and sat down.

She smiled at Joe. "I'm so glad Helen asked you over. You probably needed some friendly conversation after spending the day with those prigs Jan Reuter and Paul Clarke."

"Gram!"

"Well, it's true." She attacked some steamers, dipping them into the melted butter. She smiled at Joe again, her gaze lingering, appraising and approving.

"Hmmm. I'm thirsty," she said. "Those beers look good. May I have one?"

"Gram, you never drink beer."

"Of course I do. There's lots about me, Helen, that you don't know. You two look as though you could use another one too."

Joe Sennot stood. "Let me get them."

"Nothing of the sort. Sit right down. You're our guest." Mabel put a hand on Joe's shoulder, pushing him into his chair, and went to the refrigerator.

"Clean glasses too," she said, going to the pantry.

She hummed a happy little tune as she poured the packet of herbs she had bought from Loretta Lowell into the glasses for Helen and Joe.

Here's to love, she thought as she topped their glasses with beer, building a good head to hide any discoloration and taste the herbs might create.

The woman had her hood up because the August night had turned chilly with the wind blowing straight in from the Atlantic. The street, ancient, twisted, and narrow, was poorly lighted, but the moon made for her a vague, splotchy shadow. With her long black cloak and pointed hood, she looked to be from an earlier century.

Suddenly, her shadow was thrown against the fence beside her as headlights coming around the corner picked her up.

The car approached slowly and she saw a faint plume of her breath dance in front of her. The car passed her at a crawl and she knew she was being appraised. She could imagine the comments the driver was making to himself about her and wondered if he'd be aware of the irony of them and the logo on the car's door.

The car was a police car and on its door was the silhouette of a witch on a broom. The woman thought bitterly of how the city exploited the victims of a terrible tragedy over three hundred years ago, one of whom she was descended from. But then she thought maybe she was doing the driver of the car an injustice. Maybe he hadn't been muttering any of the usual number of slurs against her.

She had just come from a meeting with friends, others like her. Under her breath, she began to hum an air by Silly Wizard that had been playing soft background at the meeting.

The air by Silly Wizard—she couldn't remember the title—was mystical sounding and, as she got caught up in it, she looked up at the sky, at the moon and the stars and shivered with delight at their beauty, at the eternity of them. The cold wind smelled of the ocean and she liked that too.

Then she saw them in the shadows ahead of her, three of them, leaning against a wall under a tree sighing in the wind. Something about their posture she didn't like and she crossed to the other side of the street. She wished the police car would come back. She wondered why the cop hadn't rousted them for loitering suspiciously at night and then thought maybe he guessed they would harass her and wanted that to happen.

She was slightly past them when one said, "Hey, want a broom? I got a broom for you to ride."

She maintained her pace thinking, can't you at least be original?

"Oh, don't get her mad," another voice said in mock fright, "or she'll put a curse on us."

That got a little round of laughter.

"Hey, where are you going? To a Halloween party? It's too soon for

Halloween."

"Come over here. Let's see if you've got a wart on your nose."

"Or anywhere else."

More laughter.

Then they crossed the street and were in front of her, blocking her way.

"Would you please let me get by."

"Would you please let me get by," one mimicked.

"Let the lady get by, Kyle."

She placed them in their early twenties, hard, lean bodies defined by hours in a gym. She knew the type. They worshipped themselves, their musculature. They were hedonists, unthinking with no purpose but themselves and their immediate gratification.

If they were to force themselves on her, she knew she stood no chance.

"Hey, what's your name?" one said.

"I bet she's got one of them really funny names, Angie. Like Blossom or Sybil or some other stupid thing."

She didn't know whether to talk or be silent. Probably better to talk, to stall them. Maybe they'd tire of her or maybe the police car would come back.

"My name's Malvina."

"Malvina?" the one called Angie said. "That is a weird name. Hell kind of a name is Malvina?"

"It's Celtic," she said, instantly regretting the explanation and not pronouncing it with a K at the beginning, knowing the reaction the word Celtic with a soft C at the beginning would cause.

"Celtic?" Angie said. "Jesus, you guys, she plays for the goddamn Celtics."

"Stupid—" Malvina muttered under her breath.

"You say something, Honey?"

"Celtic means Irish."

"Oh," Angie said. "Hey, what you got on under that gown? Looks to me like you've got quite a lot." He came in close to her, eyeing the bountiful flesh—actually, a little too much for his taste—that the cloak couldn't hide. The others crowded behind him.

Stepping back, Malvina tried to dart to the other side of the street but they were instantly on her and she felt numbing pain in her arm as she fell to the pavement.

And then the pain came in clumps. It pummeled her shoulders, back, legs, and arms. As she turned to look up at them, a rock hit her cheek and she realized she was being stoned.

Her scream pierced the night, a long, lingering shriek that she barely recognized as her own.

More stones thudded against her and she screamed again.

Lights went on and her attackers turned and ran.

Malvina lay still for a moment and then, ignoring the inquiring voices beginning to gather, stumbled to her feet and began to run to a haven. Loretta Lowell's store was nearby and Loretta lived upstairs over it. Loretta would help a sister.

Chapter Five

When Mabel took the phone call early the next afternoon, she became an instant believer in the powers of Loretta Lowell. It was Joe Sennot asking for Helen.

She told him Helen was due in at any time and he said that he owed her a prime rib dinner.

"Can you recommend any place nearby?"

"Oh, yes," Mabel said. She could hardly wait to call Ione. She recommended two or three places known for excellence in beef.

"I'd love to have you come along, too," Joe said.

"Isn't that sweet. But beef and I don't agree anymore," she lied. "Besides, you don't need an old lady tagging along and Helen certainly doesn't need a chaperone."

"I'm at the church tidying up some loose ends," he said. "I'll call back later."

"My, my," Mabel said to herself when she had hung up. "I've got to get Ione to take me back to Salem. Hale Winters, you reclusive old painting devil, I've got you now."

Built in 1818, Madison Hall catered to all kinds of functions. North Shore debutantes usually came out in the fine old building. Those with money—the polo crowd, the yachters, and the countryclubbers—preferred wedding receptions here, even to their own exclusive places.

If the Hall were highbrow, it could also go middlebrow or even lowbrow. Over the years, many a political rally, and not just for Brahmins, had vibrated the stately old walls.

Tonight's meeting was one of the stranger ones. Loretta Lowell was holding sway over an audience of diverse mixture.

"I told you this would be interesting," Helen said to Joe Sennot. "Can you believe it, a modern-day witch talking to priests, ministers, and rabbis? Not to mention all those members of the business community. Plus a few cops and, of course, the local press."

"And a few witches and warlocks," Joe whispered. "At least I gather some are, judging from appearance."

"I'm not sure, but I don't think warlock is the correct term," Helen whispered back.

They sat near the back of the hall, having wandered over after dining elegantly on prime rib thick enough, Joe had said, to push his cholesterol count to 400.

Helen had read of the public meeting, an ecumenical getting together after a series of witch bashings, in the afternoon *Buoy* and suggested it might be of interest.

"Over 300 years ago," Loretta was saying, "this city experienced a tragic hysteria. I needn't lecture you on the causes and consequences of that hysteria except to say that not too long ago we commemorated the tercentenary of those events and many eloquent words were spoken and written about what we could learn from them."

Loretta Lowell paused. She stood at a podium and spoke into a microphone. Her voice was firm and authoritative. With that voice and her tall figure cloaked in black, she was altogether a woman of presence. The audience was attentive.

"If any one theme or message," she continued, "came from all those words, it was that of tolerance."

"Tolerance," she repeated, and let the word settle itself about the hall, her gaze following it from corner to corner.

"Tolerance, of course, allows people to be different. To look different. To behave different. To believe different."

Someone coughed. Nervously, it seemed to Helen.

"Certainly, as we all know, that message of tolerance needs spreading around the world. We could point the finger at this country or that country, at this group or that group, and we'd all nod in agreement that they could use a large measure of tolerance."

As if to punctuate that comment, several heads nodded.

"But we don't have to look around the world to find a need for tolerance. We need it right here in Salem."

Loretta Lowell paused a long moment before she resumed speaking. When she did, her voice was low.

"Last night, on one of the streets of Salem, a young woman was attacked brutally. She was attacked because of her beliefs. Because of her religious beliefs."

Glances and murmurs were exchanged.

"'He that is without sin among you, let him first cast a stone at her.' I presume you know that's from the Bible. From John," Loretta Lowell said, her voice still low.

As glances were exchanged, Loretta Lowell paused again.

"My friends," she said, her voice rising, "last night in Salem a woman was stoned, and badly hurt, because she is a witch."

Murmurs bubbled quickly into a din.

A woman whom Helen recognized as a reporter for the *Buoy* stood. "Details, please," she said.

Loretta Lowell shook her head. "There may be time for that later. For now, this person declines to publicize the matter."

She looked at the Chief of the Salem Police Department, sitting in the front row. "I will say this, however. She will be reporting the incident to the authorities."

"Wait just one minute," a male voice said. "You claim she was badly hurt. Exactly how badly?"

"She didn't require hospitalization or that type of medical attention, if that's what you mean."

"'That type' of medical attention," the voice said. "What type did she require?"

"The person came to me. I was able to administer to her some old but very effective remedies."

"Nonsense," another voice said loudly. "This whole story's nonsense."

Noises of approval filled the hall, swelling, smothering Loretta Lowell's voice as she tried to respond.

The Mayor of Salem stood and faced the hall. He was a thin, handsome man, silver hair giving him the look of a statesman. He held up his hands and waited for silence. "Please," he said, "this gets us nowhere. Believe me, Ms. Lowell, no one questions your veracity. Unfortunately, we are all too familiar with attacks over the past few months on people of the—." He hesitated, searching for a word. "—on people of the Wiccan community."

He smiled at Loretta Lowell who regarded him steadily. "In addition, there have been many other incidents. The city's witch logo on police cars has been defaced. The Salem Witches sign at the high school was destroyed. Witchcraft-related gift shops have been vandalized. Obviously, there is a great deal of hatred simmering out there. Ms. Lowell is right. Some in this city need a lesson in tolerance. Discussion only, please. No shouting. I will ask the Chief to have anyone removed who can't behave properly."

Helen nudged Joe's arm. "We can read about this in the paper tomorrow. Come on, I'll show you some of those sites."

They stood in the near dark on a hill. The moon, almost bloated, was partially covered by clouds. The east wind had come up again bringing with it the chilled air and the smell of the sea.

"Probably this is where they died," Helen said.

"There's no marker?" Joe said. No memorial?"

"There's a memorial—two, in fact. One in what was Salem Village and one here in what was Salem Town. But not here on Gallows Hill."

She pointed to a fissure in the side of the hill. "And the bodies were thrown in there. If this is the hill."

"What happened to the bodies?"

She looked at him closely a moment. "That's a mystery. We know what happened to some of them. They were claimed by the families in secret and at great risk and buried properly. Rebecca Nurse's son rowed to Gallows Hill at night. The river in 1692 came up right beside the hill." She pointed. "He got his mother's body and rowed back up the river to Salem Village and he and her other children buried her on the family property. But no one knows exactly where."

She shivered. "It's so sad. She was an old woman."

Joe drew in close to her. He pulled off his sweater. "Here, put this on. You're shivering."

"Thank you. I should have worn a jacket." She pulled the sweater over her head. "Now you'll be cold."

"No. I'm fine."

They stood very close.

"You swim in my sweater," he said. "I've got to watch my weight."

Helen pointed to another hill in the distance. "See the hill with the water tower? That's the hill most Salemites call Gallows Hill. And those cars parked down there? Probably they're just parked there with no one in them. But at one time that was a lover's lane parking spot. I guess kids today don't do that any-more, do they? I mean, not in cars. They probably go right to the main event in some motel someplace or even at home while their single parent is off some-where else doing the same thing."

Joe put his hand on her shoulder and drew her closer. She raised her lips to his.

"Hello," he said. "Someone's coming to join us."

"I don't believe it," she said. "It's Bo Monahan."

"Who's Bo Monahan?"

"Just—"

"Goddammit, Helen, what the hell's going on?" the newcomer demanded. "I saw you leaving that meeting."

Extending his hand, Joe said, "Hi, I'm Joe Sennot."

Bo Monahan stepped in, swung hard, and connected solidly. With a grunt, Joe rolled to the ground. Bo jumped on top of him, swinging and swearing. Joe swung back and connected.

"What are you doing?" Helen screamed and jumped on top of Bo. Grabbing his hair, she pulled his face around. "I said, what do you think you are doing?"

Bo Monahan jumped off Joe Sennot and looked at Helen, his eyes misting. "For chrissakes, Helen."

Joe came at him but Helen placed herself between them. "I don't believe this. For God's sake, Bo, just what do think you're doing?"

Bo Monahan blinked indecisively a moment. Then hanging his head a bit and offering his hand to Joe, he said, "Hey, man, I'm sorry. You okay?"

"I'm just great." Joe didn't take his hand.

"I got carried away."

"Yeah, you did. You've got a hot head, my friend. I don't know where you're coming from but you better go some place and count to ten."

Bo Monahan stared hard for a moment and then said, "Come on, Helen, I'll give you a ride home."

"Yeah, sure. Not tonight, I'm afraid, Bo. I'm with him."

Bo Monahan stood silently a moment, blinking in the moonlight. "Fine," he said.

They watched him run down the hill to his truck.

"I'm so sorry," Helen said. "Are you really all right?"

"I'm fine. Maybe a black eye tomorrow but I think I got him, too."

Joe began to laugh.

"What's so funny?"

"This city. This hill. Sure breeds hatred."

"I guess it does."

"Who is that guy?"

Helen laughed. "God, I'm embarrassed. Just a friend."

"Oh?"

"Certainly not a boyfriend except maybe in his opinion. I'm embarrassed to say we've gone out a few times but nothing serious."

Joe smiled and touched his face where Bo had hit him. "Well, let me get you home. Maybe sometime we can come back here and finish our discussion of Gallows Hill."

"Yeah," Helen said, kissing his face just under the eyes where a welt was forming. "It was just starting to get interesting."

Gallows Hill

Chapter Six

This time they were having pizza and a pitcher of beer at a little Italian restaurant in Stone Harbor. He had called in the late afternoon. She asked about his eye and he told her it was fine.

When Helen told her grandmother of her plans, Mabel hugged herself with delight and, if she could, would have gone immediately to Loretta Lowell's store to buy every potion that woman sold. She wondered whether she sold any to restore youth.

"Two nights in a row you're going out with him," Mabel had said. "I don't blame you, Helen. I was very impressed with Joe. I bet he earns excellent money as State Archaeologist."

"I wouldn't know, Gram."

Now as she looked at Joe while she devoured a slice of pizza sagging with lots of cheese, mushrooms, onions, peppers and pepperoni, she thought of Joe's old faded car and doubted he earned too much.

"I feel like such an ass, Joe. Again I apologize. I mean about last night. About Bo. God, you'd think he was in junior high or something. I guess I'm embarrassed because you'll think what he did is a reflection on me."

He smiled. "Certainly not. You were great. You handled him well. I think the poor guy was practically ready to cry the way you pulled his head around."

"You gave him a pretty good shot. He's probably the one who'll have the black eye. But, I just lost my temper." She touched her hair. "What a cliche I am. Red hair and a quick temper."

Joe poured more beer into their glasses.

Helen sipped from her refilled glass.

"The more I think about Bo Monahan the madder I get. Who the hell is he to follow me around and dare to presume to tell me where I go or with whom?"

She took a large gulp of beer. "That man really owes us an apology."

"He did. Let it go, Helen. Honest, I've forgotten about it. Look, let me tell you about the skeletons. They're quite old. I can't tell exactly how old but we have some further tests that will give us a pretty good idea."

"Any guesses?"

"If I had to guess, I'd say between 200 and 300 years old."

Helen nodded and chewed. That was in keeping with her theory.

"Four were men, the rest, obviously, women."

"Can you tell their ages?"

"To some extent. Within general ranges. That's more difficult with skeletal remains of former times than with those of today. Dietary deficiencies more common then—lack of calcium, for example—can mimic advanced age in a younger person."

"Can you tell how they died?"

"Hanging. They had been hanged. But this is interesting. One had been beheaded. Sorry. Maybe not so interesting while we're eating."

"Was that person a man or a woman?"

"A man."

Helen nodded and took another piece of pizza. She chewed deliberately for a few minutes.

"What can you tell about the person who was beheaded?"

"What do you mean?"

"Well, was he a tall person or a short person?"

"He was below average height."

"What else?"

Joe sipped some beer and regarded her carefully. "What are you getting at?"

"Well, to tell you the truth, I have a theory about the skeletons. When I went to the church to see Dr. Reuter and saw you and Paul Clarke, I was going to advance my theory but I guess I was a little intimidated and backed off."

"Intimidated? You?"

"Yeah. Little ol' me. But let me test my theory by asking a question. Was this headless man a strong man? Can you tell that?"

"Hmm. Interesting you should ask. Yes, I'd say he was probably very strong. He probably had a very powerful musculature."

Helen threw back her head. "Oh, wow, this is something."

"Well, are you going to tell me?"

"What you have just told me practically confirms my theory." She drained her glass of beer and topped it off from the pitcher.

"Ever hear of Cotton Mather, the leading Puritan minister in 1692?"

"Yeah. Sure."

"There's an old story that Cotton Mather had George Burroughs' head removed to study it. He thought Burroughs was the devil incarnate."

"Who's George Burroughs?"

"He was hanged as a witch in 1692. He had been a minister in Salem Village at one time but he was renowned for his physical strength. And he was below average height."

"So what are you saying?"

"When my grandmother told me about the skeletons—she heard from a friend who works at the church—I got to thinking, especially about the headless one."

"You knew about that?"

She nodded. "The number of skeletons. One headless. It added up. The people who were executed on Gallows Hill. With most of them, we don't know what happened to the bodies. They weren't supposed to get a Christian burial."

"Aw, you're just jumping to conclusions. This is probably just coincidental."

"You just said they had been hanged. The bones could be about 300 years old. Interesting coincidence, wouldn't you say?"

"You said nineteen were hanged. We don't have nineteen skeletons."

"We know that Rebecca Nurse's and George Jacobs' bodies were removed. That leaves seventeen."

"Okay. Say these are the skeletons of the hanged witches? So what?"

"So what? What do you mean, so what? Joe, you're an archaeologist. It'd be a significant historical find."

"Of course. I didn't mean 'so what' in that sense. More like in, so what do we do from here?"

Helen shrugged. "I'm not sure. I know a guy at the Stone Harbor Historical Society I can talk to who might have some ideas. I mean, maybe he could provide information about the heights and weights of the executed people that you could compare to the skeletons. Injuries or broken bones those people may have had."

Joe topped her glass from the pitcher and emptied the rest in his own, right down the middle, making a nice head of foam.

He said, "When you came to the church, you said something about the skeletons being a secret. Why did you say that?"

"It just seemed to me that a discovery like that called for some kind of official announcement. It's not as though those people had been murdered in the church, at least not recently. You know, if they were not the witchcraft victims."

"I ask because at the time I thought your comment was apt. Even though Dr. Reuter seemed very up and up as he talked with you and, before that, with me, I sensed a reluctance about the man. At first, I took it to be just the natural reaction to having anything macabre associated with the church and it might have been just that.

"But, frankly, I got the impression that it went deeper than that. I know it sounds melodramatic, but it seemed that he was aware of some awful truth about the skeletons."

"Then why would he have called you in to investigate?"

"He didn't. That came through the police. Actually, the M.E. looked at them, saw they were old, and told Chief Symmes he needed to contact our office."

"So here you are."

"So here I am."

Joe patted his lips with a paper napkin. "But the lid's off the whole thing anyway. One of the Boston TV stations is going to do a story on the skeletons and will interview me tomorrow."

"What will you tell them?"

"What I've told you. They'll play it up for what it apparently is. An interesting but harmless little mystery. No Jeffrey Dahmer here. Probably even be good for the tourist trade."

"Yeah, harmless," Helen said. She raised her glass. "Cheers."

When she pulled her truck into the driveway, she noticed the sagging old Saab parked out front. It was one of those old two-cycle engine Saabs that she couldn't begin to estimate the age of. It belonged to Mary Rose O'Brine, Ione Arrington's niece, and a classmate of Helen's. A bumper sticker said HAVE YOU HUGGED YOUR LIRARIAN TODAY?

Old foreign cars weren't uncommon in Stone Harbor and their oldness surely wasn't necessarily an indication of their owner's financial state. Old Yankee money had a predilection for old cars and old chino pants and old crew-neck sweaters with an occasional hole. It wouldn't do in Stone Harbor to be thought of as nouveau riche.

In this case, although the oldness of the car had nothing to do with eccentric old money, it most definitely had to do with eccentricity. Mary Rose, Helen thought, worked hard at being a character. Still, there had been a time when eccentricity hadn't been feigned. Mary Rose had had some emotional problems when she was younger. Overall, Helen liked her.

She killed the engine and thought of what Joe had told her. Very interesting.

She thought of Joe. Also very interesting. Last night on Gallows Hill, he had been about to kiss her until the inopportune arrival of Bo Monahan. Tonight they had eaten, talked, and gone their separate ways. But he promised to call and she had smiled encouragingly and said, "I'll look forward to it."

Maybe he had been referring to just talking further about the skeletons and for sure she wanted more about them. But she also hoped his motivation wasn't strictly archaeological and historical. Hell, if it was, she had a strategy for that.

Mabel, Ione Arrington, and Mary Rose O'Brine were sitting in the living room.

"Ah, there you are, darlin'. Home early, aren't you?" Mabel said.

Helen finger-waved and smiled at Ione and Mary Rose who finger-waved and smiled back.

"Joe had to go back to Boston," she said. Helen didn't know whether that was true because Joe hadn't said but she knew her grandmother wanted her to become romantically involved with someone of the right credentials, which meant not a fisherman. She knew Mabel probably had some kind of 1940s image of her granddaughter necking with Joe in his car somewhere near the ocean and then strolling hand in hand on the beach and eventually a sanitized, fully-clothed, old-movie consummation of heavy kissing and nothing more.

Ione and Mary Rose were regarding her closely.

"Your grandmother was telling us about that young man, the State Archaeologist," Ione said in her usual measured tones. Everything about her was measured and neat, the way she dressed, the way she sat, the way she talked. The effect was patrician. "Sounds like interesting work."

"I imagine it is."

"And he's working on the skeletons found at the church? Everyone in town's talking about them. They're fascinating."

Helen sat down on the Boston rocker beside the fireplace. The damp weather had activated the smoky smell. They used the fireplace a lot in the fall and winter and Helen liked a fire and its smell.

Mabel sat at the other side of the fireplace in a big stuffed chair. Her feet rested on the ottoman. Ione and Mary Rose sat across from them on a sofa that matched Mabel's chair. The furnishings were a mix of Colonial and Federal periods, mostly reproductions with an occasional antique. Danish modern or contemporary furniture in the old part of Stone Harbor was as appropriate as spaghetti for Thanksgiving dinner.

"I think they're going to turn out more fascinating than anyone imagines,"

Helen said. She paused a moment and wondered whether to broach her theory. The hell with it. Why not?

"I have an idea about them. As a matter of fact, I was just discussing it with Joe. I think they may be the skeletons of some of the people hanged as witches in 1692."

"Oh, dear me," Ione said, bringing her hand to her mouth a bit dramatically, Helen thought.

"That is a very interesting theory, Helen," Mary Rose said. "What makes you think that?"

Helen knew that Mary Rose had some knowledge of Salem's witchcraft history. She was a smart person, a reader. She worked in the Salem Public Library, after all. She often put aside new books that she thought Mabel would be interested in and gave her first crack at them.

Helen told them what she had told Joe. When she finished, they sat quietly a moment.

Mary Rose sipped from the coffee Mabel had served them and regarded Helen carefully through her round glasses. Helen was sure they were the same glasses she had been wearing for over twenty years, since she was a girl in grade school. Granny glasses, they were called then. And now they were back in style. They gave Mary Rose an elfish appearance, although a rather hefty elf she made. A pretty girl who liked to eat. She was a contrast to her aunt.

"If you're right, that certainly opens a can of worms," she said.

"How's that?" Helen asked.

"Well, what happens to them?"

Helen shrugged. "I hadn't given that any thought. Is it a problem?"

"Could be. The descendants might want them. To give them proper burial. I myself am descended from Mammy Redd."

"I imagine there are lots of descendants," Mabel said. "Which descendants could lay claim?"

"That's what I mean," Mary Rose said.

"The City of Salem might want them," Ione said. "Probably they would try to make a tourist attraction of them."

Helen recalled Joe's comment to the same effect.

"Ugh," Mary Rose said.

"Maybe the Episcopal Church will want them back," Mabel said. "That Dr. Reuter isn't above cashing in on something."

"Then, of course, there's this to consider," Mary Rose said. "If the modern-day witches hear about this, they might demand a pagan ceremony. They most definitely would be very interested."

"Well, it's just a theory," Helen said. "I could be way off the mark."

Mary Rose leaned forward. "Tell you what, why don't you drop by the library when you get a chance. We have lots of material on the witchcraft trials and on the people executed. We can talk about it some more and do some digging."

Helen nodded. "I'd like to do that."

As she looked at Mary Rose still leaning toward her, something caught her eye. The pendant on the chain around Mary Rose's neck had popped from under her blouse and swung loose. Mary Rose sat back and casually tucked the pendant back in.

Helen told herself that surely she hadn't seen it right. Dammit, though, it sure looked like an encircled pentacle.

All the modern-day Salem witches wore them.

When Ione and Mary Rose had left, Helen said to her grandmother, "That's a bit unusual for the two of them to be out together. Did they just drop by for a chat?"

"That and to borrow something I picked up in Salem. Ione wants it for Mary Rose."

"Oh?"

"It's not much. But it seems to be working."

"'Seems to be working'? What are you talking about?"

"Nothing, nothing."

"You're being mysterious."

"I'll tell you all about it sometime."

"Oh, Gram, you know how I hate secrets."

Mabel Waters patted her granddaughter's hand. "Come on, sit down with me and have a cup of coffee and tell all about your evening with Joe Sennot."

Salem Witch 1692 by Patty Cahill Taft

Chapter Seven

He was waiting for her on the pier when she tied up. He watched that procedure and then watched her roll the hogsheads of lobsters up the ramp. He wouldn't want to be challenged to do either.

She smiled when she saw him.

He waited while she went through her business with Charlie Goodwin and then came over to her.

"I thought I'd take a break." He jerked his thumb in the direction of the church across the street. "It's dark and musty in there and I needed some sun."

He looked at her red hair tied up in a bun. The sun dazzled off it. A thin sheen of sweat glistened on her forehead. Her fair skin had made an arrangement with the sun and the sea and had worked out some kind of tan.

"You're still working in there? I thought the bones were all gone."

"They are. Now we're into the fun part. You squat on your haunches or sit in the dust and sift and sweep one square inch at a time."

"Looking for what?"

Joe shrugged. "Who knows? Whatever might be there. Archaeology is ninety-nine percent drudgery. Just painstaking work."

They strolled off the pier. "Did you have your television interview?" she asked.

"This morning. How about I tell you all about it tonight over dinner?"

Helen smiled and nodded, her smile as dazzling as her hair.

"That sounds awfully good to me."

They had had after-dinner coffee outside on the patio of a restaurant that overlooked the wharves where two centuries earlier Salem's ships had tied up and unloaded treasures from the orient and brought fortunes to their captains.

The damp sea breeze had converted to a land breeze and the late summer's night was warm and enchanting. Now they were strolling up toward the center of Salem where Joe had parked his car.

"I told the reporter about your theory," Joe said.

"Oh?"

"You don't mind?"

"Why should I? I just thought you didn't believe it."

"I'm beginning to."

She smiled. "That's nice. The reaction of people to it might be interesting." She thought of her conversation with Ione and Mary Rose.

"Probably will be."

"I'm a little nervous about it, to tell you the truth."

Joe smiled and then laughed softly.

"What's so funny?" Helen asked.

"This town is paranoid about witches."

"How's that?"

"It just seems no one really knows what direction to take with the historical witches, if I may refer to them as that. And some of the people hanged were possibly practitioners of witchcraft. I've been brushing up on my history of 1692, I want you to know."

"Well, that's good," Helen said.

"Even with the modern witches there's an ambivalence. On one hand, the city seems willing to cash in on them if they bring in tourists. On the other, you have the witch bashing we heard about the other night at that meeting."

They walked for a few moments in silence.

"Let me tell you why I said I was nervous," Helen said. "If my theory is correct, there may be some problems I hadn't anticipated."

She told Joe of her conversation with Mary Rose.

When she had finished, they were near the Salem Common, a flat expanse about a half-mile in circumference where in past centuries livestock had grazed. Today, it was crisscrossed with cement walks and ringed with trees and benches. A cement gazebo stood near the center. They crossed to it, found a bench, sat and watched the parade of strollers and joggers.

"I suppose all that's moot until we find out if they are the bones of the accused witches," Joe said. "If we ever find out. I'm trying to get a fix on injuries recorded to any of the executed to see if they match the skeletons. But I'm afraid it might be impossible or at least inconclusive."

They were sitting close. Joe's arm was behind Helen but resting on top of the bench. His hand brushed her shoulder.

Nearby, a man was popping corn in a large enclosed cart that looked heavy enough to be pulled by a pony but there was no pony.

The gas flames glowed cheerfully and the corn popped sounding like distant fireworks. The smell was delicious.

"They say smells or aromas are the most evocative of the senses," Helen said. "Doesn't the smell of popcorn bring back all kinds of memories? Warm summer nights, like this, outside. Cold winter nights by the fireplace, snow swirling outside. Movie theatres."

Joe looked at her closely. "That's poetic. Is it a hint too?"

"Sure."

Joe went to the cart and returned with a large box of popcorn and a handful of napkins. They ate and talked. Joe's arm found its way to the top of the bench again and his hand rested more fully on Helen's shoulder.

A large brown dog of mixed ancestry sat in front of them and watched the travels of their hands from box to mouth. His long tongue lolled over white teeth and hung to one side.

"Nice smile," Helen said, nodding at the dog. She threw him a piece of popcorn which he caught deftly. He inched closer.

A siren's distant pulse grew suddenly louder and a police car rocketed by. It rounded a corner out of sight and cut its siren. Within a few seconds another followed it. From the opposite direction, sirens shrieked closer, the cars rounded the corner, and the sirens cut off in mid pulse. Blue and red light bounced off walls and windows.

People around Joe and Helen scurried to gawk.

"Want to take a look?" Joe said.

"Of course. I just didn't want to look too eager, like I don't have a life."

She threw the dog a scattering of kernels and they strolled coolly across the street and around the corner and down a small side street that led back to the water where a crowd had gathered around the police cars.

An ancient house, its gables pointing to the stars, was blazing with light. The door to the house was wide open and a woman was talking heatedly with the police.

"That's Loretta Lowell," Helen said. "That's her shop, the downstairs. She lives upstairs."

"Look at the windows," Joe said. Several of the diamond-paned windows, upstairs and down, were shattered.

"Look there," Helen said, pointing to the side of the house next to the small fenced yard.

A crude stick figure with a noose around its neck and a peaked witch's hat on its head had been spray painted on the dark brown clapboards.

Obscenities were spray painted around the stick figure and on other parts of the house.

Helen poked her head over the fence and peered around. "Look at the garden. Looks like an herb garden. Ruined."

Joe looked over and saw plants uprooted and flung about.

They watched as Loretta Lowell gestured toward something beside her front door. A plain-clothes cop bent down to where she pointed.

Helen and Joe and the crowd peered. "Looks like something smoldering," Joe said. "I think they tried to set fire to the place."

"Bastards," Helen said.

They watched for a few more minutes until Loretta Lowell and the plain-clothes cop went inside. The crowd slowly scattered and Helen and Joe headed back to his car.

"This is a strange place," Joe said. "You'd think it was still 1692. If they could, some people would hang her."

He took Helen's hand as they walked. She looked down at the brown dog still pacing beside them. She tipped the rest of the popcorn out onto the sidewalk for him and hung onto the box until she could find a trash barrel.

Chapter Eight

The Reverend Fred Whittaker of the First Congregational Church of Salem was enjoying a glass of sherry, a bit on the sweet side, and reading a history about 16th century England, albeit very informative, a bit on the smutty side. The wine was good for the blood, the old adage went, and now good for the heart, science seemed to be saying. The history was good for getting the Reverend a bit riled.

A stereo system, its CD player on shuffle, was serenading the Reverend with music appropriate to a man of the cloth and to the rectory of the old church the Reverend served.

He sipped some wine, savoring it, the music, and a passage that gave him smug satisfaction. He put the wineglass on the antique table beside him and re-read the passage. Excellent, although no smut in this part.

The passage read: No Puritan ministers were allowed to preach in Merry Old England, yet Church of England minister, Doctor Laurence Chaderton, who had converted to Puritanism in 1578, gave a sermon at Cambridge which adequately summarized the feelings of the dissidents towards the controlling Church of England. 'The Church is a huge mass of old and stinking works,' Chaderton preached, 'of conjuring, witchcraft, sorcery, blaspheming, swearing, profaning of the Lord's Sabbaths, disobedience of superiors, contempt of inferiors, manslaughterers, murderers, robbers, adulterers, fornicators, false-witness bearers and liars!'"

"What a mouthful," said Whittaker to himself. "What a wonderful mouthful and, my dear, Chaderton, it has changed little to this day." He set the book down and sighed.

The Puritans, yes, and even the Pilgrims, had come here in the 1620s to serve God and do His bidding, but the devil's disciples that Chaderton boldly chastised, slowly pushed their way into New England—God's Promised Land—and now, concluded Whittaker, had rotted it to the core. It seemed to him that he and he alone was doing something about it. He was, after all, the leader of what was once the Puritan flock at Salem. It was his duty to lead the charge against the devil and his followers. It was Reverend Cotton Mather who had shouted from his pulpit in 1692, "This is the devil's territory. His army has horribly broke upon us at Salem, which is the center and first born of our English settlements."

Whittaker idolized Mather and knew many of his sermons by heart. What a crusader he was, thought Whittaker, a man before his time. How I could use him at my side now, he mused. There are more witches in Salem now than there were in Mather's time. Not that all those hanged in 1692 were witches. Most were innocent victims. But some were practitioners of devil worship. Whittaker was confident of that. He sighed.

"And they have horribly broke upon us," he whispered to the fireplace where oak coals were glowing. There was even a witch shop on the very same street as his church. What a sacrilege. During the warm months and at Halloween tourists stood in line to get inside to buy foul ointments and pagan trinkets.

The Reverend Whittaker shuddered and his stomach turned, forcing sour bile into his throat. But he would drive them from Salem. That was his mission.

Three sharp raps from the brass knocker on the rectory door jostled the classical music and made the Reverend grimace. He put the book on the table and opened the door to a lean young man whose almost luminous smile contrasted with his swarthy skin.

"Evenin', Reverend. Mission accomplished." The young man tossed a casual salute.

"Inside," the Reverend ordered in his most commanding voice.

"Okey dokey," the young man said, not at all intimidated. He looked around, taking in the antiques, the Oriental rug, and savoring the old-church smell.

"Hey, I like the music," the young man said, still smiling.

"Spare me your irony and tell me what happened."

"Just what you wanted."

"The fire?"

"Yeah."

"I mean—"

"I know what you mean," the young man said. "It was the way you said. We didn't burn the place down. Hell, if I wanted to torch that old place, I could of done it with one match probably. Gotta be as old as the goddamn pilgrims. Dry as a bone."

"Okay, that's good. But do you think she got the message?"

"Unless she's blind."

Reverend Whittaker nodded. "You did well. I dare say you did God's work, helping me drive those heathen out of here."

"Well, she hasn't left yet, Reverend. Something tells me that dame may not be so easy to scare off. So, if, uh, any stronger measures are needed, just let me know."

"I'll let you know but for now it's best for you to lay low for a while, I think." The Reverend Whittaker took a billfold from his jacket and extracted some bills. He handed them to the young man who counted them.

"I should have been a preacher," he said. "Who would've thought? I mean you had a few more tucked into that wallet."

"Well, I may have some more work for you. God knows there are enough of the scum around."

"I'm ready anytime."

The Reverend Whittaker looked the young man steadily in the eye and then spoke in a low but firm voice. "'Be sober, be vigilant; because your adversary the devil, as a roaring lion, walketh about, seeking whom he may devour.'"

"Oh, I like that," the young man said. "Except the sober part. I suppose it's from the Bible?"

Reverend Whittaker nodded. "Peter."

"Well, Reverend, catch you later. By the way, not that you need to worry, but how do you know I did what I said?"

Reverend Whittaker patted the young man on the shoulder. "Trust. You and I are agents of the Lord. 'O taste and see, how gracious the Lord is: blessed is the man that trusteth in him.'"

The young man shook his head and smiled. "You have a good night now, Reverend."

"And you too. Good night, Angie."

Well into the second glass of sherry, there was another rap of the knocker, this one more discreet than Angie's raucous knocks. Reverend Whittaker put his book aside and went to the door.

"I didn't expect you tonight," he said, smiling at his visitor. "But how nice. Come in."

They stood by the door a moment. The Reverend put his hand on his visitor's shoulder and then kissed her lips, lightly at first, and then more deeply. As he became more insistent, she pulled away

"I need to talk with you," she said.

He waved her to a chair opposite his. "Have some sherry? It's very good."

"Thank you."

He poured sherry for her and more for himself. He handed her the glass and touched his to it.

"I'm glad you came by," he said, thinking he was glad she hadn't come by while Angie was here. "I was having an evening alone with a book. You might call it relaxing or simply dull. Probably a fine line between the two, don't you think?"

He thought of some of the passages from the book as he looked at her.

"So," he said.

She sipped some sherry, put her glass on the table between them, and said, "I imagine you've heard about the bones."

"The bones?"

"The skeletons. You know, the skeletons they found in the church foundation in Stone Harbor."

Reverend Whittaker leaned forward, furrowing his brow. "Indeed I have."

"I mean, did you see the interview on TV with the archaeologist who's working on them?"

"Yes, I did. You're talking about his theory that they may be the remains of the victims of 1692?"

"Very interesting, wouldn't you say?"

"Do you lend any credence to it? I do."

The woman shrugged. "Could be true. But how the hell did they get there?"

It was the Reverend's turn to shrug.

"Of course, the question is, if they are those skeletons from 1692, what becomes of them?" the woman said

"What do you mean?"

"Well, think of it. They could fall into the wrong hands. Become tourist attrac-

- 42 -

tions. Or . . . " She paused. "Or, who knows?"

Reverend Whittaker took a long sip of sherry and looked at his visitor carefully. His wife had died almost five years ago and he had taken solace once or twice from sympathetic ladies of his congregation and a few times from this visitor. In his view she was quite lovely. He knew some would see her as too heavy but he liked the flesh and its distribution. And the profile. Ah, it was classic. Suitable for a cameo. There was no question of her intelligence but he wasn't intimidated by intelligence in a woman. He eyed the unicorn dangling from a chain around her neck. Normally such a pagan icon would have distressed him but in her he was willing to overlook or forgive a lot.

"Let me tell you what I think should become of them," he said. I think they belong here. At this church. At the burial ground behind the church. Matter of fact, I've already been in touch with Reuter in Stone Harbor about his returning the remains to us. After all, this church—I don't mean the building— goes directly back to the original church of Salem which many of those victims belonged to."

"How did he react?"

"I don't think he was any too pleased. He was quite non-committal. I didn't press but you can rest assured I will if and when proof or strong indication comes back that in fact the remains are those of the unfortunate souls executed in 1692."

"So you'd do what? See that they got a proper Christian burial here."

"Of course. I shudder to think of those poor souls lying there stacked one upon the other for 300 years."

"Some type of very dignified ceremony?"

"Naturally." Reverend Whittaker pictured a grand-martyr funeral procession from Stone Harbor to Salem. With him leading. No doubt it would draw a lot of media attention, probably some of it national.

The woman sipped the last of her sherry but held onto the empty glass. She smiled at the Reverend Whittaker.

He smiled back.

"You're a very good man. I mean it. A very decent man."

The Reverend Whittaker smiled a modest, appreciative smile. "I try to be." He noticed her empty glass. "May I get you some more wine."

"Are you having more?"

"I'd like another glass, yes."

"Well, thank you, then."

He poured two more glasses and sat back opposite her.

She sipped from hers and then said, "Actually, I'd like some tea. You don't mind terribly, do you?"

"Of course not." In fact, the Reverend was pleased. Her drinking of tea was generally a prelude to love making. A cup of tea, a little conversation, and then hand in hand a walk to the Reverend's bedroom. The request for tea was a bit earlier than he had anticipated and he was pleased.

He went to the kitchen to prepare the tea.

Listening to the sounds of the preparation, the woman removed a packet from her purse. She felt it, hefted it as though to test its negligible weight, and then opened it.

She glanced down the dim hallway that led to the kitchen and cocked her ear for the Reverend's bustling. A tin rattled.

He'd be making that horrible domestic tea from a tea bag he bought in the local supermarket and kept in an old biscuit tin.

She went to his wineglass, poured the contents of the packet into it, and swirled the glass two or three times.

In a few moments, he came back and handed her a steaming cup on a saucer, his hand lingering on hers.

"Thank you," she said with a beguiling smile. She sipped the tea. "Perfect."

"I'm so glad you dropped by. I was feeling . . . well, you know."

"Lonesome?"

"For want of a better word, I guess 'lonesome' will do."

"No one should be lonesome." She blew on the tea.

"I try to draw on inner strength but since Marion passed on it hasn't been easy."

"You've shown remarkable strength and you've been a marvelous inspiration to your congregation."

"Do you think so?"

"I know so. I hear people talk. They say wonderful things about you."

"That's so nice of you to say."

The woman drank her tea and put her cup and saucer down. She looked at Fred Whittaker closely. Poor man didn't suspect she was a friend of Loretta Lowell, a woman he despised. If he had, they'd never have developed their "friendship."

"Finish your wine," she said. "I feel lonesome too."

He sipped and put his glass down. "I don't think I want the rest."

She got up and stood beside him. She rubbed his shoulders a moment and then picked up his wineglass. "Finish it," she said, her voice husky and low. "It . . . enhances you.

He smiled knowingly. Taking her free hand, he kissed it and then took the wineglass. He drank the liquid down and looked at the glass quizzically.

Holding her by the hand, he started to lead her down the dim hallway to the stairs.

Less than halfway down the hall, he turned, bewilderment etching his face. He started to say something and then stumbled. He fell onto his back and stared up at her.

She stared back stonily until his eyes glazed. She continued to stare for a few moments and then, with a large patterned handkerchief she pulled from her sleeve, she wiped everything that she had touched.

She finished by turning the doorknob with the handkerchief to let herself out. Before shutting the door behind her, she leaned back in and said, "Bye, Love."

Chapter Nine

The noon sun was having a little luck burning through the overcast and Helen could feel it hot on her neck. She knew this was the kind of day she could wind up with a bad burn if she wasn't careful. As she had applied SPF 15 to her neck and arms, she wished at least some of her ancestors had come from the Mediterranean.

She had pulled her traps and was about to head in when an impulse made her turn the wheel and go about hard. Despite her sunglasses, she had to squint against the glare. The sea was nearly flat and glassy, the swells languid and sullen looking. The water looked heavy.

The *Working Girl's* diesel chugged patiently as it pushed the forty footer. Helen and a cormorant sitting on a buoy eyed each other as the *Working Girl* plodded by and then the bird flew off with long, lazy swoops.

It wasn't long before Helen made the shape of Misery Island ahead, aptly named, she thought. She skirted the island and maybe a half mile past it she cut the engine and let the *Working Girl* loll in the oily-looking water.

She leaned against the stern rail and gazed about, absorbing the calm of the sea on this day. It was a trite sentiment but a true one that the sea was temperamental, she thought. One day sprite and sparkling, the next enraged and deadly, and today almost dead flat as though it were catching its energy, readying itself for some violent burst of movement and release of mood.

A sailboat sat becalmed a quarter mile away and Helen could make out a man and a woman lying flat trying to cook themselves in the rays sifting through the overcast.

Further away, a cigarette boat knifed a 50 mile an hour straight line around the far side of Misery and disappeared, its twin-engine scream a dying intrusion on the vast quiet of the ocean.

Today, as she always did when she watched other boats, whether they were sail, cigarette, or fishing boats, Helen wondered which of them under their innocent guise were bringing in a cargo of drugs. Certainly, some of those in the cigarette boats or the sailboats seemed to have money far beyond what they should. She knew some of them and she heard the stories.

And some of the fishermen or lobster men even, maybe growing desperate with the increasing difficulty of earning a livelihood from the ocean, she guessed were bringing in more than seafood.

For a long moment she stared unfocussed at the flat green-gray water. Her lips moved as if she were praying. Or talking to someone.

It was here, somewhere on the far side of Misery Island, that her father had been lost. It wasn't that far out that he shouldn't have come up somewhere eventually.

It had been a sudden, especially violent squall that had taken him. His boat, or pieces of it, had washed up on Misery and on the mainland. But John Waters had stayed with the sea. He had often said that he wanted to be buried at sea.

Helen's lips went still but she stared at the sea for a long moment more. She wondered why she still loved something, which had taken someone she loved.

She started the engine and turned about to bring her catch ashore.

Mabel served them chowder out on the little deck that Bo Monahan had built out of pressure-treated wood a couple of years ago. Bo did some carpentry on the side and was pretty good at it. He had given Helen a good price but the deck—and the good price—was a constant reminder to her of the adage that you shouldn't do business with friends. For with the deck and its low price seemed to come the subtle suggestion of some kind of obligation.

"This chowder is outstanding, Mrs. Waters. The best I've ever had," Joe said and meant it.

Mabel smiled her appreciation. "The trick's to make it not too thick. If you ask me, most restaurants ruin it by putting in too much flour."

"I keep telling Gram she should have opened a restaurant years ago," Helen said at the gas grill where she had just flipped a pound of salmon fillet barbecuing at seven minutes a side.

She sat back down beside Joe at the picnic table covered with newspaper tablecloth. Her eyes swept the small fence-enclosed yard. Perennial flowerbeds, blazing with color from May to October, ran along both sides and at the end. In the middle was a small herb garden. Her mother and father had started the flowerbeds and the garden years ago and now she and her grandmother maintained them.

A small TV sat on a table near the house and one of the network evening newscasts was on.

Joe pointed with a fork. "Listen to this, will you?"

"Salem, Massachusetts," the reporter was saying. "Over 300 years ago this small seaside community was torn by a tragic hysteria that saw 19 men and women hanged for witchcraft. Then, it was neighbor against neighbor and no one was safe from the accusations of hysterical girls. Findings of guilt were often based on virtually nothing at all, what they called 'spectral evidence.' Well, today, it seems that Salem has a similar problem. Let's go live to Salem and Fletcher Brandemeir explains."

"Thanks, Bryce," a tousled-haired reporter said as he stood on a rock near a beach. Sailboats flitted vaguely behind him in the early evening haze.

"It certainly seems peaceful as I stand here with a calm harbor behind me and pleasure craft plying the water. But this community has lately been wracked with turmoil involving some modern-day witches and we're seeing faction against faction showing an anger and intolerance reminiscent of over 300 years ago.

"It was brought to a head almost a week ago when a respected town minister was discovered dead. Police just yesterday ruled the death a homicide and, although they aren't specifically commenting beyond that, this community is rife with rumor, apparently leaked somehow from the autopsy report, that the cause of death was poison, a type known derived from herbs favored by the believers of Wicca, or witchcraft.

"Caught in the middle of all of this is Loretta Lowell, Salem's unofficial leader of its considerable Wicca community.

"Some in this old puritanical city are saying that there was no love lost between members of the dead minister's church and members of the Wicca community because it was members of this very church who over 300 years ago were involved in the accusations, tortures, and, ultimately, the executions on Gallows Hill of those accused of witchcraft.

"Earlier today we caught up with Loretta Lowell and had this interesting conversation." The reporter stared at the screen a moment until a tape of his conversation with Loretta Lowell began to run.

Loretta Lowell was sitting in her shop with an obligatory black cat huddled on her lap allowing its ears to be scratched. Loretta Lowell regarded the reporter evenly, her eyes like black marbles flashing in her colorless face.

"Ms. Lowell," the reporter was saying, "of course you're aware that the police have ruled the death of the Reverend Whittaker a homicide and some folks are saying that there was a long-standing animosity between the Reverend's church and Salem's witches."

"I know of no such animosity. I will say this, however. There certainly is a great deal of ignorance about witches and witchcraft by the general public."

"How's that?"

"Many people associate witchcraft with Satanism. Nothing could be further from the truth. We are peace-loving people who simply want to live as we wish and worship as we wish. That's not too difficult, is it? Of course, I shouldn't have to add that those rights are guaranteed by the first amendment."

"Well, that's certainly true, Ms. Lowell, but—"

"Look," Loretta Lowell interrupted, "three-hundred years ago they hanged people in this community because they thought they were witches. That was a terrible thing but place it in its time context and maybe it was understandable. Today, we're more enlightened. Ha! There are people in this community who'd hang us if they could just because of the way we look or dress or even just because of what we are called."

The reporter started to speak but Loretta Lowell pressed on. "But, hey, what do you expect in a country not too many years removed from lynching blacks or interning Japanese-Americans simply because they 'looked' like the enemy. We don't do that anymore, you might say. Give me a break. Skin-heads and creeps like them are flourishing, bashing anyone who isn't a WASP, a right winger, or a sexual straightshooter."

The cat jumped from Loretta Lowell's lap.

"Recently, a young woman was stoned by a group of 'men,' and I use the word 'men' guardedly, because she is a witch. You know, what do they think, that she rides a broom, has warts on her nose, and casts spells?"

Loretta Lowell pointed a long, white finger with a shiny, black nail at the reporter who flinched just a little from it.

"This city for years has used a stupid logo of a silhouette with a witch on a broom. It's everywhere. Even on police cruisers, if you can believe that. Well, the stupidity of the logo aside, my point is that there have been several instances of it being defaced simply because some feather brains will attack anything associated with witches."

"I've heard of that," the reporter said, sensing an opening, "and I've heard it said that perhaps it is members of the witch community itself responsible for the defacings because they see the logo as an affront."

"We do." There was a pause, long by television standards, as Loretta Lowell stared at the reporter. "The logo is an affront but believe me when I say that that kind of resolution is no resolution and it most definitely is not what we are all about.

"Let me tell you this," Loretta Lowell said as she leaned toward the reporter. "Just last week someone attempted to burn my house down. They broke windows and spray-painted a stick figure witch with a noose around its neck on the side of the house." Loretta Lowell leaned back. "We're not that far removed from 1692, are we?"

The camera lingered on her face a moment and the picture faded back to the reporter standing by the beach. "An interesting woman, Bryce," he said.

"Fletcher," the network anchor said with a smile, "I noticed you flinching a bit from Ms. Lowell from time to time. Were you fearful of a spell or anything like that?"

Fletcher laughed. "No, Bryce, but she is a commanding woman. And I'll tell you this, I don't think we've heard the last of this whole affair. Not by a long shot," he added dramatically and then paused for effect. "Reporting live from Salem, Massachusetts, this is Fletcher Brandemeir. Back to you, Bryce."

Helen shook her head. "Stupid, stupid. Big joke."

She got up and went to the grill for the salmon.

Years ago, she used to be almost like a mascot here when her father was a sergeant on the department and she was a freckle-faced little kid with her red hair tied in pigtails. Then, they had loved her, all those men in blue. Sergeant John Waters' cute little kid with a million questions and a contagious grin. They'd fingerprinted her, locked her in a holding cell, even cupped her small hand in theirs as they let her think she was squeezing the trigger on a .38 service revolver. It had all been such terrific fun.

Then the cute little kid grew into a beautiful woman who wanted to follow in Dad's footsteps. Helen became one of Salem's first women cops. For a while, there was a father and daughter team on the force but when a good buy came up on a used fishing boat, John Waters couldn't resist the opportunity to do the thing he'd always wanted since he had been a kid himself growing up in Stone Harbor.

So he left the Salem Police Department to go fishing permanently, not for fun—although it was certainly that and much more—but to earn a living doing what he truly loved. And Helen stayed on as a cop doing what she thought she loved.

But it wasn't the same as it had been when she was the cute little unofficial mascot. Some of the men who had been so nice to her when she was a little girl now acted so differently toward her. Many now looked at her as men look at beautiful women. And they behaved toward her the way men behave around beautiful women. She recognized that and accepted it. Others looked and behaved in a way that at first she couldn't understand. But it didn't take too long for her to figure it out. For a while, she accepted that too but no matter what she did, how good a cop she was, nothing could seem to overcome the resentment that some of these men felt and would always feel toward a woman intruding in what they saw as their exclusive domain.

She parked her truck in the visitors' section. This was a new modern station and all the cops now wore 9 millimeters, not the .38s like she used to tote. She still had a .38 at home tucked safely away which she took out about once a year and fired a few rounds to keep her eye sharp. New station, new guns and new cruisers but she doubted that new modern attitudes had come with those changes.

She went inside. Changes here too. Glass enclosures and high tech. Even some potted plants. She didn't recognize the young cop at the desk behind his security glass. She wondered about the security glass and then recognized that crazies could strike anywhere.

"Is Mike Doyle on today?"

"Yes, ma'am. Is he expecting you?" The cop spoke through a mike and his voice was tinny.

"No. Would you tell him Helen Waters is here, please?"

The cop pressed a button on a phone setup that had enough buttons and looked impressive enough to hook up with every head of state in the world.

"Doyle." Helen heard the voice clearly.

"Yes, Lieutenant, there's a Helen Waters to see you, the cop said and looked at Helen

"Send her down."

"Through that door ma'am. I'll buzz you through. Foot of the stairs, take a left, third office on your left."

He was waiting for her at the foot of the stairs. Still the same Mike Doyle and Helen was struck, as she always had been every time she looked at him, at how much he didn't look like a Mike Doyle. Swarthy, lean, and tall, he had the sinister good looks of someone from central casting put in the role of a Mafioso soldier. It all came from his mother's side, a nice lady Helen had met once or twice who came from Salem's small Italian community.

"Hey, partner, how you doing?" he said with a huge smile. He kissed her on the cheek and she felt the warm flush she always had felt when she had worked with him.

They stood apart, their arms outstretched, holding with both hands. "Look at you," she said. "A lieutenant. I'm impressed."

"I've been lucky."

"I don't think so. I don't think luck's got anything to do with it. I say I'm impressed, and I am, but I'm not surprised. If you don't make captain soon and chief someday there'll be something mighty wrong."

"Aw, shucks, little lady, I'm just doin' m' job," Mike said in his best John Wayne imitation.

He looked at her and smiled. "God, Salem lost its best-looking cop the day you walked out the door. Even the bad guys didn't mind being bagged by you. Bet the lobsters don't mind either. I know I'd stick my arm in a pot of boiling water for you."

She smiled back, remembering a few things about their partnership that had threatened to go beyond partnership. Actually, some had gone beyond threatening. But that was then. And now Mike had a wife and a couple of young kids and she had the *Working Girl*. She thought of Joe Sennot and wondered where that might go and then wondered whether things had to "go" anywhere.

He led her into his office. A computer, an untidy desk, a few plaques on the wall. A picture of Joe and a few other cops, some she recognized, some she didn't. A picture of his wife and kids on the desk.

He sat behind the desk, leaned back, his hands locked behind his head. She sat across from him.

"So what can I do for you? Help get you back here, I hope."

She waved her hand. "No, those days are over. It was hard enough dealing with the jerks, nuts, and deviates on the outside but when you have to take it from your own people . . . " Her voice trailed. "Well, it got to be a bit much."

"Yeah, some of them acted like jerks, didn't they? Real jerks. I can remember giving you a semi-speech about toughing it out. I guess I was as big a jerk as anyone."

Helen shook her head. "What can you tell me about the death of Reverend Whittaker?"

Mike Doyle took out a pack of sugarless gum, unwrapped it, and held it across to Helen, who declined, and then peeled the paper from a stick, bent it into a U and popped it into his mouth. He looked at Helen a moment and then said, "He was murdered."

"I know that. It was on the news. I mean—"

"Why? Why do you want to know? I mean is it idle curiosity or does the cop still live within you?"

"Look, Mike, I don't want to put you on the spot. I just thought . . . "

"Helen, you know how it is. This guy was a respected member of the community. We're playing it real close."

Helen looked at him and smiled. "'Playing it close.' That's good, Mike. Funny, but I can remember when we played it pretty loose on occasion. You were a 'hunch' guy and your hunches often played off. But, hey, I understand. This is different. You're in plain clothes now, drive an unmarked car, and I'm not a cop anymore."

"That's the way it is, Helen. Don't get sore. Boy, that Irish blood."

"I'm not sore. Even if I were still a cop, I'd probably still be in uniform and not privy to what detectives were thinking about cases, especially homicides, which are pretty hot stuff in a little burg like Salem which gets about one homicide every five years."

Mike chewed his gum a moment. "I sense a sexist thing here. An implication that just because you're a woman you wouldn't have made plain clothes. Or maybe even that if you were a male ex-partner of mine I'd open the file about the Whittaker case to you. Or . . . "

"Or what?"

"Nothing."

"What were you going to say?"

"I wasn't going to say anything."

"You were thinking that I was thinking that you were thinking that you'd tell me about Whittaker if I—how can I put it delicately?—if I put out."

"Jesus."

Helen stood and extended her hand. "Mike, I'm sorry. It was ill advised for me to come here. I did put you on the spot and I'm sorry. Hey, what say you let me buy you a pizza sometime? I mean it."

He took her hand and held it. "I'd love that. But only if it's my treat. Come on, I'll walk you up."

As they started up the stairs, he said, "I'll tell you this. The Reverend Whittaker may have been a bit more beneath the surface than met the eye. But let's have that pizza sometime and we'll talk some more."

He leaned over and kissed her cheek. "Hey, how's it going with you? Anybody regular?"

She thought of Joe Sennot, so different from Mike Doyle. "Maybe."

He smiled. "Now it sounds like you're the one playing it close."

She shook his hand and walked back to her truck in the parking lot. The bright sun and hot, heavy air was almost a shocking counterpoint to the air-conditioned gloom of the police station. She was glad she had followed her father to sea.

The woman recognized the pick up truck swinging out of the police station parking lot and heading toward Jefferson Avenue. Her eyes narrowed and she down shifted as she slowed a bit. She'd bet her last dollar that she knew what Helen Waters had been doing there. Meddlesome bitch. Once a cop, always a cop.

This would bear watching, the woman thought as she adjusted her ample weight in her seat and let the pick up pull away from her.

Yes, this would bear careful watching indeed and appropriate action if necessary. She clenched her teeth and the steering wheel tightly and then her lips parted in a grimace distorting the features of her classic profile.

Chapter Ten

She squatted outside the torn down paneling behind which the skeletons had been found. On the other side, lying in the dirt, mouth and nose covered with a protective mask, Joe Sennot toiled with a whisk broom and tiny scraper, raising little clouds of dust and, Helen thought, looking like some kind of large burrowing animal digging for grubs or insects. The mask rendered his occasional comments meaningless grunts, completing the animal image, and she responded with "umms" and "hmms" which apparently satisfied him.

She hadn't gone out in the *Working Girl* this morning, choosing instead to visit the library where Mary Rose worked to do a little research, and then visiting Joe to watch him do his archaeologist thing. Watching him didn't exactly match her pre-conceived image of archaeology, someone in pith helmet in the Gobi or Sahara on guard against ancient curses or hostile Bedouins.

"You want coffee or anything?" she asked.

She couldn't understand the muffled response.

"Huh?"

He shook his head, no, and continued to scrape and sweep. Dusty air eddied out at her. She stood, rubbed the backs of her legs to limber them from the squatting, and looked around the church basement. The church was about 300 years old and she wondered how much of it was original. From the looks, a lot.

In a corner was a metal table and a few folding metal chairs, definitely not part of the original furnishings. She opened one of the chairs and sat, spreading the morning *Globe* which she had already perfunctorily glanced at on the table.

She stared at Loretta Lowell's picture, the black and white photo doing her as much justice as any color shot would have. The accompanying article discussed the public speculation about her possible role in the death of the Reverend Fred Whittaker. Rumors flew, landed, and rolled around for examination that the Reverend had been done in by fast-acting poison, knowledge of which someone conversant with exotic substances (someone from the Wicca community, for example, Loretta Lowell, for particular example) was likely to have. Of course, the police had not yet said that Fred Whittaker had even been poisoned and Loretta Lowell had not been charged. Why the hell couldn't Mike Doyle have told her something?

Loretta Lowell may not have been charged but the mood in Salem was ugly. In his circles, the Reverend Fred Whittaker had been highly regarded and, in almost any circle, the murder of a man of the cloth was considered especially heinous notwithstanding various examples of scandalous and perverted behavior of some clergy over the past few years.

The result was that the Wicca community, long regarded with indifference or even amusement, was now under attack. Like a collection of HIV-infected black lepers, Helen thought. Actually, the attack (or attacks) had predated the death of the Reverend Fred Whittaker by a few months and, to complicate the whole matter, further rumor had it that Loretta Lowell had accused the murdered minister of implication in the assault on the Wicca community. Which, naturally, made Ms. Lowell look even more suspect in the departure of Reverend Whittaker.

Joe Sennot emerged from his dusty work, slipped the mask down, and beckoned to Helen. He had something in his hand. He held it out to her. She came in close and peered at it. Then she looked at him.

"Does it look to you like what it looks like to me?" she asked.

"If it looks like a piece of rope to you."

"That's what it looks like to me."

"Hemp, I'd say."

"You're thinking what I'm thinking, aren't you?" Helen said.

"Hangman's rope."

"Except it's too thin, isn't it?"

"Well, if that's what it is, it's part of a strand."

"Well, I'll be lynched," Helen said. "How's my little theory sound now?"

Joe lifted his eyebrows and murmured.

"You archaeologist fellas get all worked up, don't you?"

He smiled at her, his teeth white against his tan further darkened by dust. "Not usually as much as this."

"You look like one of those cartoon characters. Your face is all dusty except for where your mask was."

She looked down at the rope again. "Would a piece of rope last that long? Over 300 years?"

"It's remarkable but there have been cases. It was under some hardened sand."

"My, my," Helen said. "My, my, my. Come to my office," she said, pulling him by the hand to the metal table.

"A question: how would a piece of hangman's noose, presuming that's a piece of rope to begin with, still be around a hanging victim's neck? I mean, wouldn't they just slip the rope off the neck?"

Joe shrugged. "I don't know."

"Okay. So what do we have? Seventeen skeletons. You told me that four were men, thirteen were women. One of the male skeletons was headless. This is all consistent. Nineteen people were hanged. Rebecca Nurse's son took her body and George Jacob's body was also removed. That leaves thirteen female bodies and four male bodies unaccounted for. George Burroughs's head may have been removed by Cotton Mather. One of the male skeletons had no skull. We have a piece of what appears to be hemp rope. It all seems to add up to me."

"Seems to."

"The rope. Can you test it?"

"For what? It's rope."

"I mean for age. You know, carbon date it or whatever it is they do."

Joe smiled. "We'll test it."

"To use a cliche, this is a can of worms. You know that?"

"Yeah, you mentioned that."

"I've been doing some research. Matter of fact, I went to the library this morning. Here's a theory. Mine, but based on fact.

"First, Philip English was a member of this church. Started his own later on in Salem, by the way. He was Episcopalian and this church was. Still is. Philip English was a wealthy sea merchant who, along with his wife, had been accused of witchcraft in 1692.

"To make a long story short, they fled to New York, but when it was all over he had lost his wife—her death can be attributed to the whole ordeal—and his business had been really affected.

"So here's a gutsy guy—I mean, he really was. He held Sheriff Corwin's body, for godsakes, for ransom years after the witchcraft hysteria until he got some payment from Corwin's executors."

"Why did he hold the sheriff's body?'

"Well, it was the sheriff who had seized English's property when he fled to New York. Anyway, not only was he a gutsy guy but he must have really hated the Puritans with a passion. So, here's a guy with a big set, who hates the Puritans, who's still got some dough.

"I figure it was English who some night sails up the river which back then remember comes right up to Gallows Hill and digs up the bodies from their shallow graves and sails them over to Stone Harbor to the new Episcopal church."

"Wait a minute, I thought this church wasn't built until, what, early 1700s?"

"Seventeen oh one. Completed then."

"Years after the executions," Joe said. "You said they didn't get a Christian burial. They were probably skeletons that he dug up."

"So?"

"Just thinking," Joe said. "The skeletons here were reasonably intact. Maybe they had been wrapped or maybe he wrapped them before he transported them. We found pieces of fabric. Clothing or wrapping, I don't know. Be quite an undertaking, though, digging up seventeen skeletons and moving them like that."

"He had help, I'm sure."

"Another thing—and I'm just wondering—would a piece of noose survive all that jostling around?"

"Well, apparently it did," Helen said.

"You just want to be careful about making facts fit theory."

They sat across the table from one another. Helen reached over and brushed a piece of something from Joe's face.

"The Puritans back then wouldn't have been too thrilled with an Episcopalian being the protector of Puritan bodies. And that's where the can of worms comes in. The Puritans today wouldn't be any too pleased either with the skeletons not being returned to them."

"Puritans today? There are Puritans today?"

"The Congregationalists," Helen said. "In Salem, that's the recently departed Reverend Whittaker's church. They'd claim the victims' bodies as their own and want them returned for a proper burial in Salem. To make amends, I'd guess.

"And, of course," she continued, "the modern witches would be pissed probably on general principles. The whole thing would be a media circus. Throw in the murder of Fred Whittaker and the aspersions about Loretta Lowell—" Helen tapped Loretta Lowell's picture on the front page of the Globe—"and you don't have a can of worms, you've got a can of rattlesnakes."

"All of this is still just a theory, don't forget," Joe said.

"Maybe it's better to let sleeping dogs lie, to resort to another cliche."

"Ah, but the cat is already out of the bag, to counter cliche. My news conference. Remember?" Joe said.

"Indeed it is but sometimes if these things aren't stroked they just wither."

"So what are you saying?"

"I'm not sure. As I think it out, I don't know what's the best thing to do."

"Well, maybe it's not your choice." Joe looked at her steadily for a moment and then laughed. "For the past couple of weeks you try to convince me that these skeletons are the Salem witch victims and, now that I'm thinking could be you're right, you think maybe we should not pursue it any further. Helen, I'm a scientist. I've an obligation to follow the truth wherever it leads. You've got me going on this and I'm not about to drop it or cover it up in any way."

Helen stood. Her faced was flushed.

"Don't get your Irish up, for chrissakes."

"Don't you swear. This is a church."

Joe went around the table to her. Her hair hung long and loose. Her eyes, classic green, blazed as she regarded him evenly. She smelled good, not perfumed, but clean, freshly showered. Suddenly, he felt grubby.

"God, you're beautiful when you're angry."

For a moment she maintained her gaze and then she started to laugh.

"What's so funny?"

"I'm sorry. It just struck me funny. 'God, you're beautiful when you're angry.' For crying out loud, Joe, can't you do better than that? What cornball movie did you get that line from?"

"I mean it," he said. "You do."

"I am sorry. Don't look so crushed." She touched his arm.

"Gorgeous, actually." His voice was husky. He took both her hands and then drew her close.

They kissed, at first lightly, almost tentatively, and then each became insistent and the kiss became demanding of something more.

Helen broke away. "Not here." She laughed nervously. "We're in a church. Reuter or somebody might come down to check on you."

"Let's live on the edge," Joe said. He led her to the hole in the paneling. "In here. There's a sheet I lie on."

"Just don't say anything about jumping on my bones," Helen said.

They sat in the room in the minister's house where Helen had first seen Joe the day she came to talk with Dr. Jan Reuter about her theory on the skeletons but decided not to. Paul Clarke, the deacon was there, too, looking as wispy and ancient as ever, a virtual skeleton himself, Helen thought. She thought of what she and Joe had been doing less than two hours ago in the basement of the church next door in the dirt and dust where the skeletons had been found, only a tattered old bedsheet beneath them. After, they had gone back to her house to shower before returning to see Reuter.

When they came in, dusty and disheveled, to clean up, Helen's grandmother had eyed them, a little too knowingly Helen thought but with a peculiarly pleased, satisfied look.

Now, cleansed and smelling like soap and sunshine, they sat across from Jan Reuter and Paul Clarke.

Early afternoon sunlight filled the room, furnished with dark, tropical-wood furniture. A nice Oriental rug covered the floor. A bidjar, Helen thought. She knew a smidgen about oriental rugs.

"So you say you've about finished up with your work here?" Jan Reuter said, looking at Joe. Helen could tell he was dying to ask bluntly what she was doing here. "What a pleasant surprise to see you here Ms. Waters," he had said when she showed up at the door with Joe. Probably suspected that the connection between her and Joe was more than academic.

"Just about," Joe said. "The lab work on the bones should be concluded pretty soon, too."

"Naturally, I heard your theory about the bones in your interview on television the other day," Jan Reuter said. "Interesting."

"Actually, it's Helen's theory." Joe turned to her and smiled, his gaze and smile lingering.

"Oh?"

"Certain things added up," Helen said. "And, as I did some more research, things added up even more. But, of course, it's all still just a theory."

"What I'd like," Joe said, "is to do some more work here. Under the foundation, under the basement floor, even."

Jan Reuter blanched and Paul Clarke coughed into his fist.

"How on earth would you do that?"

"Well, we'd need a jackhammer to start but it really wouldn't be as disruptive as you might think. I'd even like to do some digging outside on the church grounds."

Both men shook their heads vigorously, Paul Clarke's strategically plastered strips of hair flying loose. He tamed and patted them back to their accustomed stations atop his shiny skull.

"Out of the question," Jan Reuter said.

"Quite," Paul Clarke said.

"I don't understand," Joe said. "You may be literally on top of a historical find of major significance."

"My goodness, man, think of the commotion, the mess. Absolutely not."

Jenny Perkins, the housekeeper, appeared on silent feet carrying a tray with a pitcher of lemonade and four glasses. She set it on a small table beside Jan Reuter and, with something approaching a curtsy, glided back out of the room.

Jan Reuter regarded the lemonade a moment but made no offer to pour. He looked at Helen. "I'm not sure I get what your interest is in all this, Ms. Waters."

"As I told you, I'm studying to be a history teacher. I like history. The Salem witchcraft hysteria always especially interested me. When I heard the particulars about the skeletons, things clicked." She explained the reasons for her theory. When she mentioned the possible decapitation of George Burroughs fitting nicely with the skull-less male skeleton, Jan Reuter seemed to squirm and Paul Clarke touched his own skull as if assuring himself it was still attached.

"We were hoping you might cooperate with us on getting to the bottom of what, as Joe said, could be a very significant find. Actually, I was wondering whether you would have anything to shed. You know, maybe artifacts or documents that you'd already come across and perhaps didn't understand the significance of."

There was a moment's silence, punctuated by shrugs and head shakings to indicate that indeed neither Reuter nor Clarke had any idea at all of any of this.

"You know," Helen said, "I don't mean to be rude, but I'm rather parched and that lemonade looks awfully good."

"Of course," Jan Reuter said. "I'm sorry."

He poured four glasses and handed them around.

"So, what do you plan to do at this juncture?" Jan Reuter asked.

Helen smiled inwardly. Reuter looked like an 'at this juncture' person rather than an 'at this point' person. "Well," she said, looking at Joe, "I guess to some extent that depends on the final lab tests on the bones themselves."

"They may be inconclusive as far as confirming the theory," Joe said. "but I've instructed the lab to list any abnormalities, breaks and so on so that we can compare to whatever injuries we can determine the witchcraft victims may have suffered during their lives."

"Even if the tests are inconclusive, something like this is going to take on a life of its own," Helen said. "It'll generate a lot of interest as I'm sure it already has started to." She and Joe exchanged looks, each remembering their little dispute in the church just a short time ago.

"So," she said, "we think the best thing to do is to follow it wherever it goes and try to discover what we can about the skeletons even though that may ruffle some feathers if they prove to be those of the victims of the witchcraft hysteria."

"'Ruffle some feathers'?" Jan Reuter said. "Do you people appreciate the— the—uproar these damn skeletons will cause?"

He took a gulp of lemonade, about half the glass, and swirled the rest vigorously, making a little lemonade whirlpool.

Paul Clarke leaned forward. Helen could almost imagine he creaked as he did so. In a crusty voice, he said, "I think our advice to you—our best advice—would be to do what you have to do, Mr. Sennot, as State Archaeologist. File whatever forms you have to, and so on. Ms. Waters, I think you should let your little theory rest. It does no one any good. Certainly not the souls those bones belonged to even if they were the hanging victims. People will talk about it for a while, as they are now, but will forget very quickly unless someone continues to feed speculation."

He leaned back and sipped from his lemonade. His hand shook but Helen suspected that was its normal mode.

Joe shook his head. "I'm afraid—"

"I'm afraid you don't know what you're getting into," Paul Clarke snapped, his voice now firm and sharp.

"Now, now," Jan Reuter said. "No need to ruffle feathers amongst ourselves." He smiled and stood. "What I think you'll find is that the whole thing is unprovable but certainly, if you or your lab comes up with anything concrete, we'll be glad to cooperate in any way we can. Short, of course, of jackhammering the basement of the church or digging up the grounds."

Still smiling, he extended his arm toward the door. "Now, Mr. Clarke and I have some matters to attend to and so will have to bid you, good day."

Paul Clarke leaned on the windowsill and watched them walk away. Across the street, the harbor glinted a cutting blue. Puffy clouds, like random sheep, dotted the sky. Altogether a scene whose beauty Paul Clarke was oblivious to.

"They're going to be trouble. You know that, don't you?" he said.

"I'm afraid so. The question is, what can we do?"

The two men looked at each other hard a moment.

"You know," Jan Reuter said, "I just wanted to get those bones back here and bury them quietly and peaceably. The last thing we need is a lot of fanfare."

"The last thing you need is someone finding out that Fred Whittaker was practically blackmailing you about those skeletons."

Jan Reuter allowed himself a thin smile. "Well, at least we don't have to worry about him anymore, do we?"

"I think our troubles might just be starting. What we've got to do now is think of a way to keep two people from screaming about those skeletons before it becomes a full-fledged media circus."

"What do you suggest?" Jan Reuter said, picking up his glass and draining it.

"I suggest we both think about it very hard. It won't be easy. You're dealing with a state official of sorts and an ex-cop." Paul Clarke leaned forward to get a last glimpse of Joe and Helen. "No, it won't be easy at all. But, you have to do what you have to do."

Chapter Eleven

Lincoln Southwick stared at the mug of dark brown beer, half full, as though if he stared long enough it would reveal something. Several mugs had preceded it. The beer was brewed on premises in the seafood restaurant that catered to both tourists and locals. The owner called the restaurant The Mainsail and the beer just Mainsail.

Across from Lincoln in the dark-wood booth sat a small, leather-skinned woman with a lot of mileage who had joined him uninvited from where she had been sitting alone at the bar. She nursed a tropical-looking drink, a mixture of juices and rum with a slice of pineapple half submerged.

She leaned across the table and in a hushed, conspiratorial tone said, "So what are you saying, Linc, that you're gonna put old Miles here out of business?"

She was referring to Miles Hackett, the owner of The Mainsail.

Linc looked up from his mug of dark Mainsail beer at her as though she was exceedingly slow, which she was. "No, not necessarily," he said very slowly and carefully, trying but failing to keep from slurring. "If that happens, it happens. That's life. Tough titty, as they say. Oh, excuse me," he said as the woman, whose name was Michele, looked offended at the 'tough titty.'

'Michele with one l' she'd always say when she introduced herself.

Linc knew the offense with the 'tough titty' was feigned. It had to be. Michele was quite loose with her own tongue. For that matter, she was quite loose with her entire body. But her coyness was just part of her act to make herself appealing. At the moment, though, Linc wasn't interested in any dalliance with Michele with one l. Maybe later. Right now, he was concerned with making money.

"There's plenty of room in Stone Harbor for another seafood restaurant. What I'm saying," he said, "is that you do it right, you can really capitalize on the tourist trade." He had a hard time with capitalize, slurring it badly.

"See, the thing is," he continued, "I figure the tourist trade is really gonna take off in Stone harbor. I mean, it's good now but nothin' like what it's gonna be."

Michele sipped her drink and then took a little nip out of the slice of pineapple. At one time she had been close to pretty but too many cigarettes, too much time in the sun, too many tropical drinks laced with too much rum, too many late hours trying to secure a man to buy her those drinks and show her some love, and, actually, too many years had taken their inevitable toll.

"How do you figure that?" she said. She wasn't really interested but she was interested in Lincoln Southwick, at least for the moment, and he definitely was interested in what he was talking about.

"How do I figure that?" Linc laughed and shook his head as though he knew a profound, secret truth.

"You know those skeletons I found at the church?" He jerked his thumb over his right shoulder in the direction the church lay across and up the street not too far away.

"Huh? What skeletons?"

"Jesus, keep your voice down, will ya?"

"Sorry. Oh, yeah. I remember. There was something about them on TV. Witches' bones or somethin'."

Linc looked to his left, out the window at the harbor glinting in the moonlight. Expensive boats, pleasure craft rather than working boats, bobbed at their moorings, some with people in them drinking and laughing. A warm breeze blew in through the screened window. Soon, the summer would be over, the water would chill and the breezes would shift.

"The way I figure it, when the word really gets out about those bones, all the tourists who go to Salem to see about witches and stuff will come flocking here to see those bones or at least the place where they were found."

He finished his mug of beer. "And maybe the guy who found them." He tapped his chest. "Me."

"So what are you gonna do, sit in a little booth somewhere with a sign that says, 'The Guy Who Discovered the Witches' Bones'?"

"No, Jesus, I told you, I'm seriously thinking of opening a little restaurant. Something I always wanted to do, actually. Sell seafood, which is always big around here, clams and lobsters and stuff, you know, but play up the witch connection. Have waitresses dress up like witches, maybe."

He looked at Michele, thinking she'd be a good candidate for the part.

"Hey, you gonna buy me another drink or what?" she said and downed the rest of the tropical mix.

"Yeah, sure." He signaled the waitress but, instead of getting her right away, two strong hands suddenly rested on the table. Attached to the hands were two brawny arms. Lincoln Southwick looked up at Lucien Thibodeau.

"Lincoln, my man. What say?" He nodded at Michele. He had bought her drinks before but it hadn't been worth it.

Lincoln nodded. In his opinion, Lucien Thibodeau was a jerk. It was best to do nothing to encourage him to sit down. Especially, he didn't want to have to buy him a drink. On the other hand, maybe he'd take Michele off his hands.

The waitress came and Lucien Thibodeau took her arrival as a cue to sit down. He pushed in beside Michele who didn't push very far, enjoying the arm to arm contact.

"Get her another of those," Linc said, "and I'm ready for another Mainsail." He pronounced 'Mainsail' as 'Mains'l' in true seaman fashion. Resignedly, he looked at Lucien Thibodeau. "You want a beer?"

"You buying? Hell, yeah." He smiled up at the waitress. "Get me a mug of Mains'l, too."

Lucien Thibodeau snugged his arm into Michele. He looked at Linc. "Hey, I overheard you talking about starting a restaurant. Where you gonna get the dough? You find a treasure with them witches' bones?"

His voice was loud and leering. He wiggled his arm around, letting it savor Michele's contours. She put hers around his shoulder. He didn't mind as long as he wasn't the one buying her drinks.

Linc was thinking what a good deal this was, buying these two idiots drinks. Lucien was amusing himself at Linc's expense and Michele was cozying up to Lucien. Not that he wanted anything to do with her but a certain principle was involved.

"So, you're gonna serve clams? Who the hell would eat your clams? You can't even cook water." He gave Michele a little jab with his elbow to cue her that he had just made a joke. He thought it was quite funny and apparently so did Michele for she joined him in a hearty laugh.

Linc was thinking maybe he'd cancel the drinks or else tell the two of them to inhale them up their nose.

"Tourists don't even know what clams are," Lucien was saying, warming to his monologue. "Look like nose boogies. Make them sick to just look at them."

"You're a classy guy, Lucien. You know that?"

The waitress came with their drinks.

Lucien Thibodeau swilled deeply from his mug. He looked Lincoln Southwick straight in the eye and said, "Thanks, Linc. Good beer. I'll tell you something, though. What I think about a seafood restaurant. No future. No future in seafood, the entire industry. Government regulations are gonna kill it."

He thought of the incident at the pier just a few days ago when Helen Waters had toppled him into the water. He had had to swim out to the jeers of friends and strangers, dripping with humiliation. "Not just the government. Certain people who don't know their goddamn place."

He became quiet, brooding into the mug of dark beer. Michele moved her hand to the nape of his neck and caressed softly. Roughly, he pushed her hand and arm aside and slid out of the booth, leaving half a mug of beer.

Linc looked at Michele and said, "Maybe you ought to go and comfort him."

"You trying to get rid of me or something?"

"You catch on quick, Michele," Linc said, slurring the words only just a little.

Angie Nolan sat behind the wheel of the Chevy Blazer, blowing smoke out the window and staring at the door to The Mainsail. Beside him sat Kyle Peterson and in the rear, leaning over between them, was Tommy Crawford. The three prided themselves on their clean Anglo looks, including Angie who, despite his swarthiness, looked more like a Nolan than an Angelo, more like his father than his mother.

They had been sitting in the Blazer for about a half-hour after leaving The Mainsail where they had occupied the booth adjacent to where Lincoln Southwick had been sitting with Michele and Lucien Thibodeau. They had found the conversation coming from that booth rather interesting.

"The sonofabitch's gotta come out pretty soon," Tommy said.

"Seeing the place is about to close, I'd say that's a pretty good observation, Thomas," Angie said.

The Anglo looks of the three actually had a decidedly Prussian cast brought on mainly by their short, militaristic haircuts. Each wore a skin-tight black T-shirt revealing a hard, sinewy torso; tight jeans; and steel-toed boots that came to mid calf. Each had a black band above the biceps of the left arm in mourning for the death of Reverend Fred Whittaker.

"Dem bones, dem bones, dem dry bones, dem bones, dem bones, dem dry bones," Angie started singing as he tapped the steering wheel. The others joined him, grinning as they sang. Angie was a riot.

"Now hear de word of de Lord," the three chorused, their voices striving for deep Afro tones.

They did another quick chorus and then sat grinning and watching the front door to The Mainsail.

"Can you imagine that shithead thinking he's gonna start a friggin' restaurant and be a big success just because he found those skeletons?" Angie said.

The others nodded their heads in agreement with Angie's observation. He was the Alpha of the trio and they were generally quick to curry his favor.

"Yeah, A real shithead," Kyle said.

"And, here he comes," said Angie. "The shithead cometh."

The others giggled a bit at 'cometh.' Angie had a way with words.

It was one o'clock and the hangers-on were straggling from The Mainsail, among them Lincoln Southwick who stepped into the night or morning, actually, and looked uncertainly around before heading to his left and up the street. His gait was like a boat on choppy water, tacking frequently and erratically.

"Poor man needs a lift, I think," Angie said. "What do you guys think?"

"Oh, he needs a lift real bad," Tommy said. He and Kyle were grinning in anticipation of some fun.

For a few moments, Angie watched Linc in his staggerings that yielded surprisingly little forward motion and then sidled the car slowly up the street after him.

"Hey, man, you look like a guy could use a couple more cool ones."

Linc paused and looked at the car, swaying a bit like a tree in the wind. He tried to focus a few moments on the driver and the meaning of his words and then recommenced his tacking up the street.

"We know a place open all night," Angie said. "Hop in, we'll buy."

Lincoln Southwick had an image, decidedly unpleasant, of an embrace leading to AIDS with the three in the car and tried unsuccessfully to kick his legs into high gear.

Angie stopped the car and nodded to Kyle and Tom. Each grabbed an arm and with little effort maneuvered Linc into the back seat.

"Hey, I saw you guys in The Mainsail," Linc said as he brought his eyes into some kind of focus on the trio.

"Indeed you did," Angie said. "A fine establishment with but one shortcoming, shared, I might add, with most all other such establishments in these parts." Kyle and Tommy were practically busting a gut. Angie was simply too much when he talked like this, exercising a fancy tongue. "It closeth too early. Why, a man barely gets started his evening's imbibing and they say it's 'last call.'"

"'Imbibing'," Tommy repeated, barely able to control himself. Where the hell did Angie come up with these words?

"But, as I was trying to tell you, we know of an establishment that stays open until the wee hours. Until the sun riseth, practically."

Linc had been preparing himself to bolt although he wasn't sure how he was going to carry that off seated as he was between two sinewy bodies in the rear seat with his own in a distinctly jello-y condition. But they didn't seem particularly threatening. And the driver, trying to talk fancy but sounding like an asshole for Linc's money, had said something about them buying. That part sounded pretty good.

"We couldn't help overhear you talking with your friends in The Mainsail," Angie was saying. "So you're the guy discovered the skeletons, huh? You think they could be the witches' skeletons?"

Linc managed a shrug. "That's what people are saying."

The Blazer was trolling the street slowly, probably no more than ten miles per hour, a reasonable but never observed speed considering that the street was scarcely wider than a driveway and was as winding as a country stream.

"Now, the church is around here somewhere, right?"

"Guy's asleep, Angie," Kyle said.

"Wake him up."

Kyle and Tommy shook and jostled Linc for a few moments before his eyes opened. "Jesus, he's drooling," Tommy said. "I hope he don't puke."

Angie had pulled the Blazer to the side of the street. He leaned over and looked at Linc. "Hello, there. We were talking about the church. Remember? The church where you found the skeletons."

He waved his hand slowly in front of Linc's eyes. "Hello, there. Wake up." His tone was soft and friendly.

Linc's head lolled to the side, almost on Kyle's shoulder.

Angie's hand shot out and grabbed Linc's chin. He held and squeezed. "The church?"

"Just up the goddamn street. I tol' you already."

"Yeah, you told us."

Angie put the Blazer in gear and headed up the street.

He started humming, Dem bones, dem bones, dem dry bones, again.

"Hey, I thought we were going to get a drink," Linc said.

"We are. First, I just want to check out that church," Angie said as he parked the Blazer across the street from it. The church was dark except for a light glowing from the basement window.

"So, that's where you found the bones," Angie said.

Linc grinned. He really wanted another beer or two but he didn't mind strutting his stuff a little about his discovery.

"Yeah, right there near the front of the basement." He pointed. "I was working on the foundation. I'll tell you, when I first saw 'em . . ." He paused, trying to think of some appropriate image that would convey the enormity of his feelings at that time. "It was really something," was all he could think to say.

"So where are they now? They still in there?"

"They were sent into Boston, I think, to be examined. But I think they might be back by now. Reuter wants them buried here."

"Who's Reuter?"

"The minister."

"Oh, yeah, that's right," Angie said.

"Matter of fact, he wants me to build the caskets."

"So, you think they might be back?"

"Maybe. Hey, how 'bout those beers?"

"Yeah, yeah," Angie said. He opened his door and motioned to the others. "Let's go take a little look around first."

"Nothing," Joe said, emerging from the hole in the wall.. "There's nothing else to be found. I mean short of digging up the whole floor."

"You're lucky he let you back to do this much," Helen said. She was sitting on one of the metal chairs she had pulled in close to the wall. She yawned and punched Joe lightly on the arm. "Come on, let's go. Let's pack it up." She looked at her watch. "It's way past my bedtime."

They had come back earlier in the evening after Joe had talked with the lab and was told that one of the skeletons was missing two finger bones. It was skeleton nine. Female. Could be significant if they learned that a hanging victim had been missing fingers on her right hand. But the first thing, obviously, was to see whether Joe had overlooked them at the church.

At first, when they came back to talk with Reuter about doing some more work in the basement, the frostiness of the afternoon hadn't thawed. It was obvious he suspected a ploy that would allow Joe to start tearing up the basement floor.

"Look, Dr. Reuter," Joe had said, "I just want to dig in the dirt a little more where I've been working all along. Believe me, I respect that this is your church. You don't want me digging up the basement floor, I'm not going to do it. Besides, I start with a jackhammer and you'll know it."

That had been earlier. Now he said, "God, I'd love to be able to tear up this floor. That man is an idiot. An obstructionist."

"Tsk, tsk, you shouldn't talk that way about a man of the cloth."

Joe brushed off his shirt and pants and wiped dirt from his face. With his chin, he pointed to the space beyond the hole to where the sheet covered the dirt. "What do you say? Up for another tumble in the dirt?"

"My, my," Helen said. "How blase and direct we've become. What happened to, 'You look beautiful when you're angry.'?"

She moved in close to Joe, brushing his collar and then his shirtfront. She put her arms around his neck. "What are we going to do after tonight when we can't use this place. It's so kinky. I mean, it's so forbidden."

Joe pulled her closer. "Well, we can always visit churchyards at midnight."

They kissed for a moment and were starting to crawl through the opening when Helen stopped. "What's that?" she said.

"What's what?"

"Shhh." She cupped her ear and cocked her head.

"I don't hear anything," Joe said.

"I did. I heard something."

"Like what?

"Like someone up in the church. We better not go in there. It's probably Reuter or Paul Clarke coming to check on us."

They both stood still and listened.

"It could have been anything," Joe said. "A mouse. Maybe a squirrel."

"Maybe."

He drew her close again and nuzzled her throat. "C'mon, loosen up. It wasn't anything."

They kissed and crawled back into the wall. Joe spread and smoothed the sheet. They lay together, mouths and hands busy, breathing deeply on the lumpy, centuries-old dirt that had just recently couched seventeen skeletons.

Suddenly both sat upright. "I heard it that time," Joe said. "That wasn't any squirrel."

They crawled from the hole, buttoning as they did.

Joe grabbed his flashlight. "I'll go up and check."

"I'll come with you."

"You wait here. It could be vandals."

"Stash that 'wait here' stuff. I used to be a cop. I can handle myself."

Joe snapped out the basement light and they climbed the now darkened stairs from memory. The noise had stopped.

The door at the head of the stairs opened at the front of the church to the left of the pulpit. Joe put his hand on the knob and listened. Blackness and silence.

"Open the door and take a look," Helen said. "Use your flashlight." She pushed his arm.

A sound, footsteps, maybe. A scuffing.

Then, no mistake now, footsteps coming toward them.

Joe opened the door and stepped out. Light from the street dimly illuminated the pulpit and rows of pews.

A shape slammed into him, knocking him to the floor. He swung his flashlight and struck a shoulder but was rewarded with a fist to his jaw.

Then Helen was on Joe's attacker. From her police days she had learned there are no rules in this kind of situation, no fairnesses, no gentility.

She used her nails, working nails, on strong working hands, on his neck and the side of his face. When he turned toward her, she drove her knee into his chin.

He fell off Joe and tried to roll away from her. She grabbed Joe's flashlight, a long torch, and swung it like a club into the man's head. She swung it again and this time it broke.

"Sonovabitch," the man said and rolled to his legs. He looked at Helen as if pondering a charge but instead turned and ran to the back of the church. Two other shapes scurried out with him.

Helen turned to Joe. "You okay?"

He was squatting, rubbing his chin. "I'm okay. But you're plain terrific. You really are."

He got to his feet and came to her.

"Come on," she said. "Let's see where they went."

They ran toward the front of the church. Near the door, Helen stopped. "Whoa. What's this?"

She bent down, picked up a gasoline can, and shook it. It was full. She opened it and sniffed. "The bastards," she said.

They went outside, looked around, and then darted toward a figure sprawled in the bushes near the sidewalk.

Helen knew it would be a night of little sleep. They had called the police and were now talking with one of them, a guy in chino pants and a checked short-sleeve shirt. Jan Reuter and Paul Clarke, looking like a couple of characters from a previous century in their pajamas and robes, stood with them. Helen half expected they'd be wearing nightcaps.

A uniformed cop was walking Linc Southwick back and forth on the side-walk. It was Linc who had been lying in the bushes. Beyond being held firmly by John Barleycorn, he was unhurt.

The lock on the church door had been easily broken but there was no damage inside the church.

"Yeah, we were just buttoning things up," Joe was saying, "when we heard them upstairs."

The 'buttoning up' made Helen want to jab him in the ribs with her elbow.

"And there were three of them?" the plain-clothes cop said. He was one of Stone Harbor's few plain clothesmen.

"We saw three," Helen said.

Jan Reuter looked sharply at her. "You two were there late enough," he said. "You told me you had just a little more digging to do. My God, look at the hour."

The cop, whose name was Pappas, said, "Look, Dr. Reuter, I don't mean to butt in, but these people probably saved your church from being burned down."

"Yes, yes, I appreciate that." He gave a curt nod to Joe and Helen. "Thank you."

Helen flashed a cold smile.

The uniformed cop came over. "Lieutenant," he said, "Linc, here, maybe has got some information about what happened."

Linc Southwick wavered a bit uncertainly in front of the group, looking from one to the other. His face brightened and he smiled when he saw Helen.

He mumbled through his story, starting with spending some time at The Mainsail but skipping over his idea of opening a seafood restaurant. When he described the three who picked him up and how they had inquired about the skeletons, Jan Reuter and Paul Clarke shifted nervously.

"Did they assault you?" Lieutenant Pappas asked.

Linc grinned and shook his head. "Damned if I can remember, George. I was pretty far-gone anyway. That home brew they make at The Mainsail is mighty potent stuff."

Helen could tell that George Pappas would have preferred being called

'Lieutenant' in these circumstances. That was the thing about a small town, everyone knows everyone else.

"Okay, Linc, thanks a lot," Pappas said. "Whyn't you go with Officer McDonald here. He'll give you a lift home."

He turned to Helen. "So, you think you might have marked one of them?"

"Oh, yeah. I drew blood. These nails may be stubby, but they're sharp. I'd say I got him pretty good on the cheek and neck."

"You should have seen her, Lieutenant," Joe said. "I'll tell you, I was impressed. She got him pretty good in the face with her knee too. That guy couldn't get away fast enough."

Pappas appraised Helen. "I'm not surprised. Helen was pretty tough as a kid and then as a cop. And she can haul traps with the best of them, I've heard. I know this is—what do they say?—politically incorrect, but Helen's one tough broad. No butch. Christ, I don't mean that. Far from it. Damn nice looking, if I do say so."

"Geez, thanks, George. If I ever need a reference or anything, you wouldn't mind, would you? I mean, the 'no butch' part would really look good."

"Aw, for crying out loud, Helen, lighten up. You know what I mean."

"The 'damn nice looking' would also be helpful. Think maybe you could work something in like, 'real mean body?' Course, I don't know, maybe I don't merit it."

"She's tired, Lieutenant," Joe said.

"Jesus, you too, Joe?" The phrase 'Et tu, Joe? Then fall, Helen' flashed before her and she started to laugh.

"Watch your language, please, Ms. Waters," Jan Reuter said. "We're in front of a church."

"Oh, sugar," she said and walked away.

Within a few minutes, Joe caught up with her. "Calm down, calm down," he said.

They walked in silence for a moment.

"Like you said, I'm just tired."

"Pappas didn't mean anything," Joe said. "He was just being complimentary in his own way. His choice of words maybe could stand some improvement. And I sure as hell didn't mean anything. I suppose you think I was being condescending."

"A bit."

"Well, I wasn't. But you did come on strong to the guy."

"Okay. I'm sorry. Chalk it up to whatever cliche you want. Temperamental woman. PMS. I'm having my period. Touchy broad."

"That'd be the same as temperamental woman."

She turned to mock punch him and he ducked away.

"Easy, easy. That's not the way I want to connect with you."

He came in close and put his arms around her. They hugged and kissed a few moments. "Joe, we're on a public street," she said, pulling away.

"Yeah, but it's two a.m. No one will see us."

"Dream on." She started to walk.

"Well," he said, keeping pace with her, "Pappas said we'll have to come by the station tomorrow and finish giving our statement."

"Uh huh. Just a thought but I wonder if these bozos are the same ones who tried to burn down Loretta Lowell's place."

"The way Southwick described them they sound like skinheads. Could be witch bashers, I suppose, although it doesn't make any sense to bash bones, if that's what they were looking for. And why burn the church? None of it makes any sense."

"Those kind of people make no sense," Helen said. "They're just haters. They hate Catholics, blacks, gays, Jews, and, it seems, witches, historic or modern."

A car zipped by, too fast for the street.

"And, I'll tell you this, too," Helen said. "Those guys probably scared the day-lights out of Reuter and Clarke. If they get their hands on the bones again they'll bury them before anyone knows what's happened. What time are we supposed to go to the station tomorrow?"

"When we get a chance."

"Good. I'll go in the afternoon. I've got to haul traps in the morning. I can do that with the best of them, you know."

Chapter Twelve

She worked in a boutique that specialized in fancy linens and sweet-smelling soaps. It was located on what had been, a couple of centuries ago, a busy wharf when Salem had been a thriving seaport with her ships sailing all over the world and bringing back fortunes.

Today the wharf had been urban renewed. It had a winding road, streetlights that looked like gas lamps, and upscale shops and restaurants.

Helen had gotten her name from Mike Doyle and getting it had been like getting a four-year old to share his ice cream. Finally, he had said, as they sat in his office at the Salem Police Station, "You didn't get this from me, Helen." He handed her a slip of paper with the name Malvina Drinan on it and Malvina's home and working addresses.

Helen had looked at it and said, "I'll commit this to memory and then swallow it, Mike. If I'm questioned, I promise I'll use my cyanide capsule."

He had thrown a paper clip at her and told her to get lost. "Remember," he said with a leer, "you now owe me. Big time. But let me tell you this too. This Malvina Drinan is no saint. There's stuff about her that, let's just say, if I were you, I'd watch my step."

"Yeah? Like what?"

"Hey, I've said enough. Just be careful."

That afternoon, after bringing the *Working Girl* in, she had gone to the Stone Harbor Police Station and finished her statement to George Pappas. Then, after seeing Mike Doyle, she tried Malvina's home address, a small apartment off Salem Common. Like just about everything in this part of the city, it was old. Some of Salem's old houses carried their years well. This place didn't.

When she rang the bell, a series of frantic, high-pitched barks grew louder and closer on the other side of the door and she could hear the dog's nails as it danced and sang at her. From the tone of the barks, she knew it was a small dog. After a few moments, the barks became growls, and then barks again as Helen talked to the dog through the door.

"Calm down, sweetheart," she said. "I'm a nice person. You'll like me when you see me."

She was about ready to leave, when she heard footsteps coming toward the door. "Be quiet, Tara," a man's voice said.

The door opened and Helen looked at a small dog with curly white fur. A pink bow was tied atop the dog's head. Tara stopped barking to sniff Helen's shoes.

The man, about thirty, had on chino shorts, a T-shirt with a Tall Ships logo, and no shoes. He needed a shave.

"Hi," Helen said. "I'm looking for a Malvina Drinan."

"That right? Good luck."

"She does live here, doesn't she?"

"I suppose," the man said. "Hey, Tara, get outa there." With his bare foot, he pushed the dog away from Helen's sneaker.

"That's okay," Helen said. "I don't mind her."

"Yeah, Malvina lives here but she's hardly ever here, know what I'm saying? Like, I might not see her for two weeks straight then all of a sudden she's here all the time. I haven't seen her in, I don't know, maybe a week." He scratched his cheek and looked at Helen closely.

"You a friend of hers?"

"No. I just wanted to talk to her."

"Well, I don't know what to tell you. I mean, you could try later on. It'd be fifty-fifty if you'd see her. Less than that, probably."

"Okay. Thank you."

"Any message."

"No. I'll catch up with her."

She left Tara and her friend, thinking they were a cute couple, and walked to the wharf where Malvina worked. She didn't want to ask Malvina questions at work but Tara's pal made it pretty clear that she didn't have much choice.

At the boutique, she hovered around a counter of scented candles for a moment breathing in phony garden smells while she waited for the salesperson she had pegged as Malvina to finish with a customer. She had Wicca written all over her, from her sun-shy skin to her Indian-black hair. The main clue, Helen thought, was the unicorn hanging from her neck.

When the customer left, Helen went to the counter. She smiled her warmest smile and said, "Hi, I'm looking for Malvina Drinan. I understand she works here."

Pale eyes studied Helen a moment. "I'm Malvina."

Helen eyed the other clerk, a woman who looked to be in her early sixties, carefully coifed and dressed, the antithesis of Malvina. "Is there a place we could talk a minute?"

"What about?"

"I think you could help me. I want to ask you about the men who stoned you."

The pale eyes looked Helen up and down. "Are you a cop?"

"No. I'm a fisherman and lobsterman. Or lobsterwoman or lobsterperson if you prefer. My name is Helen Waters. I'm from Stone Harbor."

The eyes flicked to the coifed woman and then back to Helen. "I'm due for a break. Wait a second."

She went and spoke to the coifed woman and then came back to Helen. "We can go outside."

They sat on a bench under a locust tree, its lacy leaves scattering the sun.

"You said I could help you. How?"

"I have reason to believe that I may have run into the same cretins you did. I was hoping you could describe them to me."

Malvina brushed a strand of black hair from her face and compressed her lips. Helen judged her to be in her mid twenties. Too much weight and Wicca coloration and starkness didn't diminish a pretty face. Her profile was quite lovely, Helen noticed. As she studied her, she thought she looked familiar and wondered if she had known Malvina from her cop days. If she had, the chances were good that wouldn't bode well for Malvina's character. She wondered what Mike Doyle had meant when he had advised her to be careful with this woman.

"They were animals." Malvina's eyes filled a little and she worked her mouth some more. "I thought they were going to—to—you know, rape me at first. Then they started throwing rocks at me. Can you believe that? They stoned me. I thought they were going to kill me. All I could think of when they were doing it was the story "The Lottery." Did you ever read it?"

"Yes. By Shirley Jackson."

Malvina pushed up the sleeve on her left arm. Above the elbow a healing gash puckered from a surrounding blue-gray blotch that stained the white skin. "I thought they broke my arm." She touched her thigh. "They got me here too. And you should see my back. Bastards. I'm lucky they didn't hit my head. They did get my face but I had a hood on and it protected me. I don't think they ever saw my face."

"It must have been awful," Helen said.

Malvina looked at Helen as though checking her for bruises. "You say you ran into them? Did they attack you?"

"Not exactly but I have reason to believe they may be the same people. How many were there?"

"Three."

"Did you get a good look at them?"

"Not really. Not close up. Just a general impression from a distance before they—before they started. I'd say they were in their early twenties. They looked strong. You know, as though they lifted."

"I know the type."

"They looked like skinheads, I guess. Shaved heads. Tight clothes. Boots."

Helen nodded. "Sounds like my boys. Guys you'd like to get close to."

"Yeah, so you could do a little non-anesthesia surgery."

Helen laughed and Malvina joined her. They shook together on the bench a moment savoring the thought of some strategic slashing.

Helen held out her hand. "Well, if it makes you feel better, I got one of them pretty good in the face with my nails."

Malvina smiled. "Good for you. Oh, by the way, I got a name, too."

Helen's eyes lit up.

"Two names, actually. Angie and Kyle. Angie seemed to be the leader."

"Angie and Kyle," Helen repeated. She wondered whether they had called each other by real names.

"I gave the names to the police. What will you do?"

"I don't know. Try to see if they match up with the guys I ran into. Then...?" Helen shrugged.

She extended her hand and Malvina shook it. "Thanks very much for your time, Malvina. By the way, that's a beautiful name. I love it," Helen said, meaning it. "I'll let you know if I have any luck."

"Be careful," Malvina said. "I think these guys are capable of anything. Of the worst."

"Well, that means we can't just sit back and let them get away with their dirty stuff, doesn't it?"

"Wait here a minute," Malvina said. She went back into the boutique and came back out clutching something. She handed it to Helen.

Helen looked at the small pin and then at Malvina quizzically.

"It's good fortune. But you have to believe." Malvina regarded Helen carefully as though to see whether she would mock the pin.

"Thank you very much," Helen said. Again, she tried to place Malvina from her cop days.

She walked away, the pin clutched in her hand, and wondered whether maybe it was time to start carrying some stronger luck. Like the .38 tucked away at the top of a closet at home.

After a quick pick me up of a non-fat strawberry yogurt, a plum, a piece of Entemann's no fat marble cake, and a glass of skimmed milk (rationalization for cholesterol and saturated fat later in the evening if she saw Joe and they ate as they usually did), she went back out to find Lincoln Southwick.

She knew where to look. About this time, Lincoln would be starting his evening at The Mainsail, eating a clam roll and getting a leg up on his ration of beer.

He glowed when he saw her and, when she sidled up to the bar beside him, he practically became fluorescent.

"About last night," she said, getting right down to business.

He smiled, taking her in, savoring their mutual involvement in something, even if it meant the police.

"Hey, let me buy you as beer," he said. This was something: Helen Waters sitting beside him at the bar of The Mainsail.

"Sure. Linc, this is important. Can you remember the names of the guys you were with last night?"

Linc stared at her, the smile slowly fading as he thought of last night. For a minute, all he could remember was sitting at the booth with Michele and Lucien Thibodeau.

He shrugged. "Geez, Helen, I guess I had had one or two too many. I don't think I even heard them use any names."

His smile returned as he studied her. She smiled back and patted his hand. Instead of mentioning the names Malvina gave her straight out, she decided to try a verbal line-up.

"Linc, see if any of these names ring a bell."

He nodded, the smile broadening to a grin.

Okay. Here we go. Just listen to them all before you say anything. Ken. Sam. George. Bill," she said, giving about a three seconds' pause between names. "Mike. Fred. Paul. Kyle."

She wished he'd wipe that shit-eating grin off his face.

"Jay. Angie. Steve. Jarrod."

The grin had disappeared.

"I can remember," Linc said. "I can remember one of them saying I was asleep. But I wasn't. He said, 'Guy's asleep, Angie.' Yeah, that was the name he used. Angie."

Helen patted his arm. "You did great, Linc. One other thing. What kind of car were they driving?"

"Oh, hell, I don't—It was one of those things like a Jeep but not a Jeep. Bronco, Blazer, something like that. Hey, don't you want your beer?"

"Some other time. I mean it. You have it for me."

Good work. One other bar tonight. In Salem, this time. Try to see Mike Doyle for the second time in a day. He used to stop at a particular waterfront bar for a couple when he got off duty. She checked her watch. He should still be there unless there had been a change of habit. Matrimony could easily do that. She had stopped there with him a few times. She thought about that as she drove.

She parked out front on the narrow street that a couple of centuries earlier had been the focal point for big-time international commerce.

Mike Doyle was at the bar with another guy she didn't recognize. She motioned toward an empty booth and, with a quizzical look, he said something to his friend and joined her.

"Twice in one day, Helen? Not that I mind."

"Yeah. I was thinking the same thing. People will talk."

"What's happening?"

"First, thanks for Malvina Drinan's name. I talked with her."

"And?"

"And she gave me a couple of names."

"Uh huh."

"By the way, you said she might be trouble, remember? Would I have known her from my days on the force?"

Mike Doyle shrugged. "Could be. She gave you names?"

"Yeah. The same names she gave to you. An Angie and a Kyle. No last names."

Mike Doyle nodded and sipped his rum and Coke.

"Any progress in locating them?"

Mike Doyle shrugged.

"See, this is what bothers me," Helen said. "I'm sensing something here I don't like."

"What would that be, Helen?"

"Indifference. I mean, she gave you guys descriptions and names but so far you've got nothing."

"How do you know what we've got?"

"Tell me you've got something. Tell me you've questioned these guys."

"For chrissake, she gives us a couple of first names which may or may not be genuine and descriptions that could fit a lot of guys."

"Not so many. Salem's not that big. Here's what I'm thinking, Mike, and

- 73 -

you're not going to like this. We've got a woman who has been assaulted—not sexually—in a pretty odd ball way. I mean, stoning isn't your assault of choice these days. But the thing is, she's an odd ball. She's a goddamn witch. She got what she deserved. Odd ball assault on odd ball person. So you guys go through the motions but who gives a damn?"

"Hey, what the hell's all this to you anyway?"

A waitress hovered. "A draft beer," Helen said without looking up.

"What's this to you?" Mike repeated.

"I think I met up with the same guys last night in Stone Harbor."

"Whoa. They assaulted you?"

"No." Briefly, she told him what had happened, leaving out the part about the witches' bones.

"So what do the Stone Harbor cops say?"

"They're checking. They'll probably at least half try, seeing that a church is involved. You know, I wouldn't be surprised if these were the same guys who tried to burn down Loretta Lowell's place a few days ago."

Mike Doyle swirled his drink and stood up. "Helen, I gotta be running. Nice seeing you."

She grabbed his arm. "Wait a minute. Give me a minute, will you? Sit down."

Mike Doyle sat but his gaze was hard. "Look, Helen, we go back, but I gotta tell you I don't much care for this 'you cops don't give a shit because it's a woman' routine. That's crap."

"Where can I find these guys?"

"Hey, look, I don't know who they are and if I did I couldn't tell you. You know that. Besides, what would you do?"

"Come on, Mike, this is me. Helen. As you say, we go back. I'm not going to 'do' anything. I want to know, though, who it was that nearly cooked us."

"This archaeologist. You say he was doing a dig for artifacts. Witches bones, right? I mean everyone's talking about it. He was even on TV. You and he an item?"

"He's a nice guy."

The waitress put a glass of draft in front of Helen. Mike slipped her some money before Helen could react.

"I'm a little jealous of the archaeologist," he said.

"Don't talk nonsense."

"I'm not." He put his hand toward hers, fingers touching fingers. She drew her hand back.

He looked at her wistfully a moment and then said, "You're okay, Helen. There are some guys we've been watching. Skinhead types who match up to the jokers you're talking about. For the most part, they seem to be hanging out up on Route 1 in one of the sleaze motels but they've been hanging around Salem a lot. Keeping some strange company, too. Seemed to be close to the late Reverend Whittaker, if you can believe that. Strange bedfellows, huh?"

"Which motel?"

"The Sunset. When they're in Salem, they spend a lot of time in the Wet Spot

- 74 -

drinking beer and pinching asses."

Helen nodded and they sat a moment. Then she said, "Let me buy you a drink. I think one should support her local police."

Malvina Drinan sat in her darkened living room and thought of her conversation that afternoon with Helen Waters. The pungent smell of burning incense filled the room.

Of course, she had recognized Helen right away and was surprised that Helen hadn't recognized her. Or at least she seemed not to. But she supposed that a cop dealt with so many people that she couldn't remember them all. Probably only the worst and Malvina certainly had never done anything so terribly bad that she'd fall into the category of the worst.

Besides, that had been a few years ago and she'd been a bit slimmer. Quite a bit slimmer. She had hung at some wild places with some wild people and done some wild things but never anything felonious. All before she had discovered Wicca and some very nice but misunderstood and, hence, persecuted people.

She sighed. Nothing was ever easy.

Her thoughts drifted back to Helen Waters and she knew they'd be in touch again before long. She'd see to it.

As she thought of the good fortune pin she'd given Helen, a broad smile spread over her face and she breathed deeply of the perfumed air.

Chapter Thirteen

"You ask me, I say break their friggin' legs. For starters," the woman said. Originally from New Jersey but a resident of Salem for several years, she was one of some fifty witches from various parts of the U.S.A. and Canada gathered at Loretta Lowell's place in a show of Wicca solidarity. As many as could were jammed into Loretta's living room. The rest spilled into the adjoining room.

It was stifling. The warm early afternoon air from the outside fluttering in through cranked out diamond-paned casements was enriched by body heat. Incense and faint perspiration concocted a pungent perfume.

There was a murmur of yesses and no's at the woman's pronouncement, a nodding and shaking of heads.

"And I can get the guys to do it. Bonafide hard asses, let me tell you." They all looked at the woman. She was reputed to have Mafia connections. Her name was Felicity.

"Hear, hear," Loretta Lowell said. "That's no way. You know we're not about violence. Violence begets violence."

"Very true, very true," Felicity said. She was heavyset but her eyes were almost as sharp and her presence almost as commanding as Loretta Lowell's. Her profile was classic. "They started the violence and they'll be getting it back."

A ripple of laughter rewarded her pun. Even Loretta Lowell smiled. "It's tempting, I know. But, really, it's not the answer. You all know that. We don't want to make things worse."

"Well, that's why we came to Salem," Felicity said. "To help our brothers and sisters. We've been hearing some disturbing things."

"They'd like to drive all the witches from Salem," Loretta Lowell said. "Make money from 1692, preach about intolerance, but drive us out. Hypocrites."

Loretta Lowell looked around at her gathered Wiccans. Perspiration beaded her forehead and upper lip. "Mainly, they're after me. It's no secret that the police suspect me in the death of Fred Whittaker," she said, for the first time that evening touching upon that sensitive topic. "But, unfortunately, the rest of you, by association, also pay. So not only do we have to contend with the kinds of idiots who tried to burn down this place, but also with an antagonistic police department."

She looked Felicity directly in the eye. "I appreciate where you're coming from, but, again, I can't emphasize enough that violence isn't the way. But that doesn't mean we roll over and let the bastards push us around. What we do, I think, is we help each other. We travel in pairs. And it wouldn't hurt to carry Mace." Loretta Lowell smiled. "Or a more potent potion, if you have one."

Some smiles and head noddings followed this.

"Now," Loretta Lowell said, "why don't we go outside where it's cooler and there's more room so that we can all join hands in a circle and ask for help for us now and for peace in the world."

When the circle broke up and they drifted their separate ways, many in groups of at least two as Loretta Lowell had suggested, Mary Rose O'Brine walked by herself to her old Saab.

She checked her watch. She wondered what her friend and classmate Helen Waters was up to since she had come into the library a couple of days ago. Helen might be in from her day's lobstering. Maybe she'd drive over to Stone Harbor and pay her a visit. Be nice to see Mabel too.

Helen wasn't home but, surprise, a young guy was visiting Mabel Waters. Even at a quick glance, he appeared sensible, dependable, and wholesome. And not at all bad looking, Mary Rose thought. She recognized him at once for she had seen his interview on television about the bones discovered at the church. This could prove very interesting. She was glad she had come.

Mabel fluttered about, beaming as she made the introductions.

Mary Rose and Joe Sennot shook hands.

"Joe's Helen's friend," Mabel explained, with a wink and just the slightest emphasis on 'friend.' "Course, I don't imagine you thought he was here to see me."

"Of course I'd come here to see you," Joe said. "Especially if I thought there was some of your clam chowder in it for me. She makes absolutely the very best clam chowder I've ever had. And I mean it."

"I've had it. And I agree," Mary Rose said. She leaned forward. "So, Joe, these bones you've been studying. They've made quite a stir. What can you tell me about them?"

"What would you like to know?"

Mary Rose's eyes were wide. "Well, are they really the bones of the Salem witches? I'm sorry, I should have said, the bones of those executed for being witches?"

"We're not sure yet. We may never be sure, actually."

"Oh, you're being cagey. Come on, you can tell me. He can trust me, can't he Mabel?"

Mabel wagged a finger. "Enough about old bones. That's what we're all coming to anyway. Just a bunch of old bones."

"Where are the bones now?" Mary Rose asked. "God, I think this is so interesting"

Joe fidgeted. "Well . . . "

Mabel grabbed Mary Rose by the arm. "You come out here and I'll give you the recipe to my chowder. Joe, you just make yourself comfortable right there. Helen should be along any minute. There's a great book I'm reading about mummies right there beside you. Take a look at it. You should find it interesting."

In the pantry, Mabel squeezed Mary Rose's hand enthusiastically. "I have got just the most exciting thing to tell you," she whispered. She paused dramatically and then gestured with her thumb back toward Joe in the living room. "Isn't he just great? Respectable looking. Handsome even. And an archaeologist. I think that is terribly exciting. A Yale man. Or was it Harvard? One of those. Doesn't matter which, does it? Can't do much better than Yale or Harvard, can you?"

Mabel raised her voice. "Cream. You want to use heavy cream. Bad for the arteries but there's no substitute for the taste."

Back to the whisper. "As you can no doubt surmise, he's terribly interested in Helen. Hopelessly in love, I would say. And, if I know my granddaughter, she's just as in love with him."

Loud voice: "Dice the clams. But not too small. You want something to sink your teeth into."

Whisper: "Here's the most interesting part." She reached into a cabinet and pulled out a small packet. "This stuff is an absolute miracle." She gave it a little sniff and proffered the packet to Mary Rose to do the same. "Herbs."

"Oh," Mary Rose said, sniffing the packet. "For the chowder?"

"No, silly. This is a love potion. And don't you dare laugh. Guess where I got this."

Mary Rose shrugged.

"In Salem. From Loretta Lowell. I've been using it on Helen and Joe and you can see the result. You might think I'm just a silly old lady, but I'm sold on it. Tell me, I know it's none of my business, but do you have a young man you have your eye on? You are certainly welcome to some of this. Actually, I can't see where you'd need any, you're such an attractive girl, but then again, so is Helen. Sometimes it helps just to give things a little shove."

Loud voice: "Cook slowly. Good things are never rushed."

Mabel winked at Mary Rose as she spoke. "Except sometimes we help them along, don't we?"

She poured a glass of beer for Joe and sprinkled some of the herbs into it, swirling the glass a bit until the powder dissolved.

"Here, now, " she said to Joe as she handed him the glass. "Have a cold beer while we wait for Helen."

After drinking the beer, declining another, and making stilted, evasive conversation with Mary Rose, Joe walked to the wharf saying that Helen was late and maybe needed some help unloading or tying up.

He sat on a bench in the shade and watched the unloadings and listened to the comments about declining catches and hard times now and ahead.

He recognized the guy he had a scuffle with on Gallows Hill leaning against a pickup and talking with a couple of others. He tried to think of his name. He went through the alphabet once and started again. B. Bo. He had it. Bo Monahan. He grinned as he thought of the incident. Really adolescent situation but Helen had been great. Actually had popped Bo right in the jaw. Then he thought of her in the church going after whoever it had been in there. What a woman. And beautiful to boot.

He waited another fifteen minutes and was beginning to get concerned when he spied the *Working Girl*.

She came in and tied up perfectly, making it look easy.

When she handled the hogshead and rolled it up the ramp, he smiled broadly.

She spotted him and smiled but he thought she looked embarrassed. As she went through her thing with Charlie Goodwin, Joe watched Bo Monahan and some of the others. They were watching Helen carefully and Joe saw something smoldering there that he didn't care for.

When she and Charlie had finished, she turned to Joe and he went to her.

She held up her hand like a traffic cop. "Don't get too close. I warn you, a day in the sun, playing with lobsters and fish, is more than any soap, perfume, and deodorant can handle."

"You are Woman," Joe said, kissing her cheek. "And you look and smell great—under any condition."

"O-o-o-o-e-e-e," a voice said mockingly. "Give her a real kiss, for chrissakes. If you know how."

"Ignore it," Helen said.

Joe looked over at the guys leaning jauntily against the pickup. "Was that Bo Monahan?"

"It wasn't Bo. It was that asshole, Lucien Thibodeau," Helen said, making no attempt to keep her voice down.

"I heard that," Lucien said, stepping forward.

"You probably hear it a lot," Helen said. "That ought to tell you something."

Joe stepped between them. Lucien eyed him contemptuously, taking in the pleated chino shorts and buttoned-down shirt. He rolled his shoulders, the muscles rippling under the dark blue T-shirt. "Hey, who's Mr. Brooks Brothers, here?"

"Look," Helen said, "why don't you go find some junior high kids somewhere and throw a few flexes at them, maybe make a few smart-ass comments, make that pig call you just did. You'll fit right in. You could probably even become their leader."

"Hey, nobody calls me an asshole."

"Look at you," Helen said. "You're a grown man but you make cat calls and now you're standing around rolling your shoulders and flexing your arms. You didn't think that 'Mr. Brooks Brothers' comment was funny, I hope."

"Listen—"

"No, we're not going to listen. Now, run along like a nice little boy before you make a complete ass of yourself."

Lucien Thibodeau rocked indecisively on his heels a few moments. He worked on a face-saving sneer, looked back at his friends, and then shook his head sadly as if he and the rest of the world knew he was dealing with idiots. "You two deserve each other."

"Great comeback," Helen said to Joe as Lucien walked away. "We were really put down."

"What is it with the guys around here?" Joe said, as they walked off the wharf. "You certainly seem to bring out the animal in them. 'Course, in a way, I can relate to that."

She punched his arm playfully. "I beg your pardon."

"It's true. All the men act as though they're in rut when they're around you."

"Including you?"

Joe smiled. "Well-l-l . . . "

They crossed the street. In the yard of the church they saw Paul Clarke attending a shrub. He looked their way, ignored Helen's wave and averted his glance.

As they walked past, Helen spoke. "Hello, Mr. Clarke."

He looked up from the shrub with its gorgeous purple blooms, and smiled a thin, watery smile. "Why, uh, hello."

"Pretty flowers," Helen said. "A Rose of Sharon?"

Paul Clarke seemed flustered. "I wouldn't know."

Helen nodded. "They're late bloomers. Actually, it's best to prune them in the spring."

Paul Clarke mumbled and snipped a branch with small pruning scissors.

"Have a nice day," Joe said.

"Warm man," Helen said when they were out of earshot. "Probably, I shouldn't have zinged him on the best time to prune the shrub. But, anyway, what were you doing at the wharf?"

"I'd been waiting for you at your house. Had a nice conversation with your grandmother who seemed intent in getting me drunk, by the way. Kept trying to ply me with beer."

Helen laughed. "That's funny. Gram's not usually one for booze, either drinking it or serving it. I notice now, though, there's always beer in the house and she always makes a point to serve you some. She really likes you. I can tell."

"I also met your friend Mary Rose O'Brine. She was really curious about the skeletons."

"Mary Rose was there? She never comes by during the day."

"I couldn't tell her much. But, anyway, you were late so I thought I'd stroll down to the wharf to wait for you and see if you wanted to take in a movie or something tonight."

"Sounds good but before we do, how about taking a spin with me tonight up to the Sunset Motel on Route 1?"

Joe smiled and pointed with his thumb back at the church. "A sheet and the dirt in the church basement weren't good enough for you, huh?"

"Listen, Bub, a sleazy motel is the last place I want to make whoopie. But it might be home sweet home to the guys who tried to burn down the church."

"So we're going to play detective?"

"Oh I'm not playing," Helen said. "I'm not playing anything with these guys."

Paul Clarke watched Helen and Joe walk away. Angrily, he snipped another branch. A Rose of Sharon indeed. Best to prune it in the spring. Damn know-it-all.

He dropped the pruning scissors beside the little pile of branches under the shrub and strode to the minister's house where he found Jan Reuter reading by a window.

The two spoke animatedly for a few moments. Jan Reuter leaned out the window to watch Helen and Joe as they walked away, his brow furrowing.

He pulled his head back in and regarded Paul Clarke evenly. "I quite agree," he said. "They've gone far enough. It's time to put a stop to it. It won't be pleasant but I don't see where there's any other choice."

In approaching darkness, dusk coming early in late August, they drove to Route 1 on a crowded, straight road past illuminated malls and upscale car dealerships selling Acura's, BMWs, and Lexus.

Joe turned his old Mercury Zephyr wagon—he called it an archaeological relic, something he dug up from a previous civilization—onto Route 1.

"The Sunset's about a half mile up the road," Helen said. Just swing through the lot first. We're looking for a Bronco or Blazer."

"Then what?"

She shrugged. "First things first."

The Sunset was shaped as a tipped L with the office and a few units on the bottom of the L and bulk of the units lined up as the top of the L.

Joe pulled past the office and a Vacancy sign and slowly cruised the parking lot. There were seven parked vehicles, none of them a Blazer or Bronco or anything of that genre.

"The Sunset does a booming business," Joe said. "Real fancy spot. By the way, what makes you think they're staying here?"

"I have my sources."

Joe made a U-turn and stopped. "Now what? No Broncos, Blazers, Pathfinders, Rodeos, or any off-road vehicles, for that matter."

"We can't sit here. Pull up in front of the office."

"Won't we look obvious?"

"If the manager comes out, we're mulling whether to stop here for the night or to continue north a bit further. We have the right to mull."

"You don't mind my asking what you plan to do if these guys show up, do you?"

"I just want to get a look at them. Hard to proceed without knowing who you are proceeding against."

"'Proceed'?"

"Yeah. Proceed."

"Right."

Joe tapped the steering wheel, accompanying a little tune he softly whistled. Helen slouched, turned against the seat, so that she could view any vehicle coming in off Route 1.

After about ten minutes, Joe said, "Check this."

A man and a young woman, not much older than a girl, actually, came out of a unit about five doors down. He was wearing light blue pants, white belt and white shoes and a dark shirt. She was barely covered by a sundress.

"He's definitely AARP and she might be out of high school," Helen said.

"Aw, you've got an evil mind. The Sunset wouldn't allow that kind of thing to go on."

After another five minutes, Joe said, "How long do you plan to keep this vigil?"

"Just a while longer."

"I'm getting a bit hungry."

"So am I." Helen looked at her watch. "It's 7:45. We'll give them 'til eight, how's that?"

"Oops. Might not have to wait at all," Joe said. "Isn't that a Blazer just pulling in?"

They watched it drive almost to the bend in the L. Three men got out and went inside.

"Pay dirt, I'd say," Helen said. "You check out the bandage on the neck of the driver? I knew I got him good."

"You sure did. So now we eat?"

"Not quite. Got to figure a way to get a closer look."

Joe groaned. "I figured you say that."

Twenty minutes later, they were back out and into the Blazer.

"Follow 'em," Helen said. "But stay back."

"No problem with this thing," Joe said, patting the dashboard.

The Blazer went north on Route 1 about a half mile before it turned off.

"Good thing," Joe said. "I could never have stayed with them if they stayed on the highway."

They drove through a winding road overhung with tree branches, the homes well-kept, many of them very old but nicely restored. Lights glowed softly in windows and cars were snugged in driveways.

"This is where the witchcraft hysteria started," Helen said. "Today this is Danvers but in 1692 this was Salem Village." She pointed to the left. "Back there, off the road, is where Samuel Parris's parsonage was. You know, where his slave Tituba told the girls of Salem Village tales of voodoo or whatever. That's really where it all started."

"I'd like to check it out sometime when we're not play-acting a B movie script."

The Blazer, about 200 yards ahead of the Zephyr, took a swooping left. They followed it through Danvers center and then lost it when Joe hit a red light.

"Damn," he said. "Should I run the light?"

"No. We'll be all right. I can still see them."

When the light changed, Joe kicked the Zephyr hard.

"Don't panic," Helen said. "Small town cops hunger for speeders. It's their reason for being. Even if we lose them, I've got an idea where they might be going anyway."

"Then why go to the motel and do all this tailing?"

"I said I've got an idea but I'm not positive. Besides, look at all the excitement you're having."

They picked the Blazer up again at another set of lights. Joe pulled up four cars behind. They maintained the tail into Salem and followed the Blazer to a public parking lot. Joe stopped across the street opposite the parking lot.

"They're probably going to the Wet Spot. It's just up there." Helen pointed to a place where light and noise spilled out to the street. A cluster of choppers was pulled to the curb in front of it.

"Classy looking."

"It's a joint. They'd fit right in. See? There they go."

They watched the three get out of the Blazer and swagger, bandy-legged, toward the Wet Spot. They laughed and punched one another's shoulders and arms.

"They're like junior high kids," Joe said. "Socking each other, probably telling dirty jokes."

"If only they were that innocent," Helen said, watching the three go into the Wet Spot

"Okay, Nancy Drew, what's the next step?"

"Pull into the parking lot and we'll let them get settled. Then, what say you and I mosey on in and have ourselves a drink? I gotta tell you a couple of things, though. One, you won't find Sam, Rebecca, Norm, and Cliff in there. Two, don't use a glass. Drink your beer from the bottle."

"Reminds me of the place in one of the *Star Wars* movies," Joe said. "Remember the scene with Hans Solo and all those weird critters? Looked like a bunch of trolls and ogres."

"This place is not nearly as charming."

They sat at a table in a row of tables between booths and the bar. At the far end of the bar, the three from the Blazer stood and swilled beer from bottles. They were talking and laughing with a couple of guys seated at the bar who looked like their soul buddies, like storm troopers: short haircuts, sleeveless black T-shirts, and tight black jeans.

Staccato sounds—frenzied screams and strident instrumentation—blared from the jukebox. Smoke hung in a haze, replenished continuously. It seemed as though everyone in the Wet Spot but Joe and Helen was smoking.

The walls were decorated mainly with framed posters of 70s hard-rock stars. On the wall behind Helen and Joe was hung a picture of mixed animals in trench coats and fedoras—dogs, cats, a pig—seated at a large table playing cards. A Harley-Davidson logo hung over the bar

The Wet Spot was crowded. Every stool at the bar, every booth and every table was taken. Joe and Helen had to stand and wait ten minutes before their table had been vacated. Now they sat with a bowl of salted peanuts and two open bottles of beer and empty glasses in front of them and kept their eyes on their friends from the Blazer.

"Be a good place to study the effects of second hand smoke," Joe said. "Or excessive decibels."

He tilted his bottle, took a deep swallow and set the bottle down. He touched his button-down collar. "I don't think we're dressed appropriately. As a matter of fact, I detect a few contemptuous sneers, if I'm not mistaken."

"It's not contempt. It's jealously."

"Right. By the way, do we have a game plan here?"

"No."

"Okay. So we sit and stare, blacken our lungs, damage our eardrums, and probably run the risk of AIDS just by being in here. I'm for that."

"You exaggerate. We'll just tinge our lungs a little, suffer only temporary deafness—a couple of days maybe—and end up only HIV. No way full blown AIDS. Now be still and be patient. See what happens. One thing I was curious about was whether they'd recognize us. Obviously, they don't."

"Jesus. What if they had."

"Oh, stop it. I had every confidence that you could handle them if they got belligerent."

Joe rolled his eyes and sniffed. "You know, that's not just cigarette smoke in the air. And I don't mean Borkum Riff."

"Oh, I know."

"The cops ever come by here?"

"Sure. But mainly when there's a fight, a stabbing, or someone starts swinging a chain or something. Which happens fairly often. Or at least it did when I was on the force."

"You think any of these *Australopithecus robustus* recognize you as a former cop?"

"Any of these what?"

Joe smiled and waved his hand in dismissal. "Just a weak archaeologist joke."

"They might."

They sat and worked on their beers. Helen peeled at the label on her bottle with a fingernail. The waitress, tight jersey, tight jeans, a lot of hair, and hoop earrings large enough to double as bracelets, came by and looked inquisitively at them.

Joe held up two fingers. "Sure, why not?" He munched some peanuts and proffered the bowl to Helen.

She shook her head. "Too salty."

"That's the only thing keeping them fresh. Oops. Our friends are scoring."

The three from the Blazer had slid into a booth.

"Two gorgeous creatures. Not my type but nice in a drag strip kind of way."

"Just two?" Helen said. "I wonder who'll be third man out."

The bandaged one, his back to Helen and Joe, sat with one of the women and his two friends sat with the other between them. They drank, smoked, talked, and rubbed into one another for several minutes. The one on the end got up and fed the juke box and a few minutes after that the bandaged one got up and went to the men's room. It said STUDS on the door.

"I bet the graffiti is really clever in there," Helen said.

"Can you read what it says on the ladies room door?"

Joe squinted. "I think it says BOARDS. Figures. They can't spell. Supposed to say Broads."

Helen shook her head. "No. Think about it. Studs fit into boards."

The waitress returned with their beers and Joe paid her. In a couple of minutes, the man came back out and slid back into the booth.

"Obviously, he's the leader," Helen said.

"How can you tell?"

"He doesn't share a woman. Notice the other two didn't hit on her while he was gone? Generally, they defer to him."

"Brilliant."

"Elementary."

"Oh-oh," Joe said. "One of them is staring at us. I think he's made us."

The three were looking hard at Helen and Joe; the bandaged one swiveled in his seat.

"Don't get into a staring contest," Helen said, smiling. "Just act casual." She laughed as though Joe had just said something funny.

"Just be aware of them peripherally. If they don't make a move, we'll sit here a couple of minutes, finish our beers, and then leave to see if they follow."

"I'll say this," Joe said, "you know how to show a guy a good time."

They forced phony laughs and smiles and a casual, relaxed drinking of their beers. The three at the booth kept their eyes on them but seemed unsure.

"Okay, we're out of here," Helen said. "Just get up, walk out and don't look at them."

They went to the parking lot and sat in the Zephyr. "Should we wait a minute?" Joe asked.

"No. They're not coming. If they were going to follow, they wouldn't be subtle."

Joe looked at her, trying to keep the exasperation from his expression and voice. "What the hell did we accomplish by all this, Helen?"

She smiled sweetly. "We worked up a hell of an appetite, didn't we? At least I did. Let's go eat."

Mike Doyle called her the following morning as she was about to leave for the wharf. "Can the lobsters wait a while this morning, Helen?"

"What's up?"

"I'd like you to come to the station for a few minutes, if you could."

"It can't wait? It's supposed to get rough out there later on."

"It might get rough here, Helen."

"Beg pardon?"

"Look, Helen, you're a friend so I'm handling this a little bit different than if I didn't know you. A whole lot different. Ordinarily, I'd have a cruiser over there to give you a ride in."

"Mike, you're being a tad obscure here. I have no clue what you're talking about. Spell it out, will you?"

"Two nights ago we had a little chat, remember? About three guys. I give you the motel where they stay and the joint they hang in. Last night you follow them from said motel to said joint. You and a male friend were seen in the same joint. Reports say you have words with the three men. Early this morning as the three leave the Wet Spot, one of them tumbles to the sidewalk flat on his face."

"Stop it."

"Guess what? He's dead. It's too early to know for sure but my guess is he was poisoned. And I wouldn't be the least bit surprised if it was the same shit that did in the Reverend Whittaker."

They sat in Mike Doyle's office. Helen had on her work clothes: jeans, a sweatshirt, and ankle-high work boots with non-slip soles. Her hair was in a ponytail.

"Here's what we've got, Helen. Deceased's name is Angelo Nolan. From Charlestown. Post mortem's scheduled this afternoon."

"P.M. this p.m., huh?"

"Helen, I gotta tell you, this ain't funny. You could be in deep shit. I'm doing you a favor. This isn't exactly procedure, you know, talking to you like this off the cuff."

"I'm sorry, Mike. I appreciate it."

"Nolan's friends, a Kyle Peterson and a Thomas Crawford, also from Charlestown, claim that you and a male companion followed them from Route 1 to Salem. I assume the male companion is the archaeologist?"

"You know, Mike, maybe it would be better if we weren't off the cuff. Maybe I should call a lawyer?"

Mike Doyle shrugged. "Any way you want it. I haven't charged you with anything. I'm just talking to you, Helen. You know what I'm saying? I'm trying to be up front with an old friend and partner."

"What's this about my having 'words' with these three guys?"

Mike Doyle drummed his fingers on his desk and then rubbed his chin. "Peterson and Crawford claim you walked by where they were sitting on your way to the ladies room and said . . ."

Mike Doyle took a pad from his desk and looked at it. "They say you looked at Nolan and said, 'How's your face feel? I'm going to give you a real taste of something.'"

"Oh, cut it out, Mike, will you."

Mike Doyle leaned back. "You didn't say that?"

"Yeah, I walked by them, said that, and then said, 'give me your drink so I can put some cyanide in it.'"

"But you were at the Wet Spot."

"Yeah, I was at the Wet Spot. And, yeah, I followed them from their motel."

Mike Doyle leaned forward suddenly, the spring in the swivel snapping loudly. "Jesus Christ, Helen, thanks a lot. I told you about the motel and the Wet Spot in confidence. You said you weren't going to do anything. What the hell have you gotten into?"

"I wanted to see the guys who tried to light up the church in Stone Harbor. With me in it."

Mike Doyle did a complete clockwise swivel in his chair and then looked at Helen for a long moment. He did another swivel, counterclockwise this time, and looked at Helen some more.

Then he stood. "Let's take a ride," he said.

Even when she was a cop, she had never been to the morgue.

Mike parked behind the hospital. He rang the bell by a door at the basement and showed his badge to the young man who answered.

"Like to see male Nolan, please. He was brought in early this morning."

The young man consulted a clipboard and nodded. He led them to a drawer halfway down. The fluorescent lights and pale green walls were a combination to make even the living look dead, Helen thought. She expected a smell but there was none.

The attendant slid the door open and a sheet-covered body stretched before them, the sheet lumped at the feet and face.

Mike slid the sheet back and Helen looked down at the face of Angelo Nolan. She had seen dead people at wakes and, as a cop, newly dead people, faces and bodies torn and twisted inside cars also torn and twisted. She had seen a man battered by the bricks he had fallen onto from a church steeple. Once, she had stared at the bloated, puckered body of a young woman who had been in Salem Harbor for almost a week before she washed up onto some rocks and ruined the beach day for a lot of people. The fish had been at her.

But she had never before looked at reposed death, death unretouched by the undertaker's art where hair is washed and combed and color is added to lips and cheeks.

Angelo Nolan lay in the ultimate vulnerability, unable to present himself as he may have liked, indulging whatever vanities he may once have had. Bruises marked his forehead and nose. The left side of his face still bore the three furrows where Helen's nails had done their work.

Mike Doyle looked at the attendant and motioned with his finger that he wanted the attendant to leave them by themselves with Angelo Nolan. The attendant nodded and walked away.

"He one of the three guys you followed to the Wet Spot?"

"Sure is. He's also one of the guys who tried to torch the church." She held up her right hand showing Mike her nails. "I got him good, didn't I? The sonofabitch. Sorry. Probably shouldn't have said that."

"Said what? That you 'got him good' or 'the sonofabitch'?"

"He's also one of the guys who attacked Malvina Drinan."

She looked at Mike Doyle. "Okay, Mike. I've identified him. I've admitted I gouged him. I've admitted I followed him to the Wet Spot. But I most definitely did not threaten him. Now what?"

"Now we leave. You go pull up your traps and I wait for the M.E.'s report and proceed from there."

Mike Doyle pulled the sheet back over Angelo Nolan's face and signaled to the attendant.

When he dropped Helen off by her truck, he held her hand and patted it. Then, his voice serious and almost sad, he said, "If I have to talk to you again about this, Helen, I'm afraid it won't be off the cuff. At this point, I don't want to sound too ominous, but you might be thinking about a good lawyer."

She did her traps with an eye to the sky. The clouds had thickened and those to the northwest looked as though they might be building to thunderheads. Some were starting to show the sharp edges of boomers. The sea was still flat but she knew she should head in soon. Actually, she should have headed in a while ago.

Correction on that, she thought. She shouldn't have come out at all. To boot, she was developing a headache, a fitting companion to the blackening sky. Probably from not having any coffee this morning. And from her talk and little excursion with Mike Doyle.

The whole incident was really peculiar and troubled her. She had thought she knew Mike Doyle well but now she was beginning to think she couldn't figure him.

It didn't look good, her and Joe's following those three from Route 1 and being seen at the Wet Spot just before Nolan died. Well, not just before. Not by a long shot. And that was the thing. There was no case at all against her or Joe. Just innuendo, the kind of thing that can hurt reputations and distress those close to you (like Mabel Waters) if it gets out that the police are checking on you, somehow linking you with a crime, with a murder.

Maybe it wasn't a murder at all. Maybe Angelo Nolan had had a heart attack or a stroke. It could happen. Maybe the guy had done a line of coke and sent his ticker into uncontrolled spasms. That definitely could have happened. Angelo and his cohorts for sure didn't look like strangers to illegal substances.

So where was Mike Doyle getting off? Did he know something beyond what he had told her? What really bothered her was a feeling she couldn't shake, that in some kind of twisted, perverse way he was trying to hit on her.

She had two traps to go. A sudden gust of wind hit her and the *Working Girl* rocked as the sea picked up. She looked at the sky. Dangerous to push it. Time to get in.

The traps would have to wait. Mike Doyle had ruined her day big time.

Reverend Cotton Mather

Chapter 14

The woman with the classic profile sat in the lotus position in the middle of the floor of a darkened room. Soft, almost tuneless wind-instrument music played and incense thickened and spiced the air.

But the meditation wasn't working. Too many thoughts intruded, disturbing thoughts, like wasps and flies that will not be waved away from the food on the plate.

To begin with, she was not an evil person. Most assuredly not. She had had to do what she did simply because there was no other way. She had been genuinely fond of the Reverend Fred Whittaker and looking into his dying eyes had been like looking into the eyes of a euthanized animal (she had done that and it was the most ineffably sad thing she could think of) and watching the light of life fade and cloud over.

The young man called Angelo had been easier but still not easy. True, he had been an ignorant, violent no-good, a sybarite of the lowest order but he was a person. Best not to dwell on that. At least she hadn't had to look into his dimming eyes.

She timed her breathing. Slowly, deeply breathe in, hold for a half second, and slowly release. Experience both the sensuality and spirituality of respiration

She repeated her mantra, thinking it, timing it with the breathing in, not sure whether that was recommended technique but not caring because it had always worked that way before.

Breathe in and think, Love. What purer ideal was there?

Hate. Hate could be even more purifying in its way if it cleansed, and, if it did indeed cleanse, it could lead to love.

She hadn't hated Angelo and most certainly she hadn't hated the Reverend Fred Whittaker but she had hated what they might have brought about.

Not the time to think about all of that. Now it was time to drive all thoughts away except, Love.

Through her nose, she breathed in, her heavy bosom rising as her lungs swelled with air. She thought, Love, trying not just to see the word but to feel the concept, to let its soothing balm strengthen her.

Breathe in not just air but Love itself.

Breathe in, Love.

Breathe in, Love.

She had it. It filled her, driving away Reverend Fred Whittaker and Angelo Nolan, blocking her senses to incense and music. She was aware of nothing but Love.

For several moments she was Love until an intrusion like an insistent buzzing wasp couldn't be ignored.

Like the Reverend Fred Whittaker and the non-reverend Angelo Nolan, one more troublemaker remained to be dealt with.

As she thought about it, as Love slipped away, one comforting thought at least remained: Dealing with Helen Waters should, if anything, be easier than the other two. She knew just how she would do it.

The local papers carried only small columns about the death of Angelo Nolan of Charlestown and did not indicate that the police suspected foul play. Helen had to wait until the following day for the obituary to run in the Boston *Globe*.

It was a brief three-liner in the unpaid obituary section but gave her the piece of information that would serve as a starter: the name of the funeral home.

The wake would be just this afternoon and tonight. That would give her plenty of time to work her traps, get back in, have a leisurely supper, freshen up, and drive to the Sullivan and Conlin Funeral Home in Charlestown to pay her respects.

Charlestown is the section of Boston where the Battle of Bunker Hill (or Breed's Hill) was fought. On top of the hill, towers a monument, resembling a small Washington Monument. Not too far away, as the crow flies, in the old Boston Navy Yard the U.S.S. *Constitution*, "Old Ironsides," floats regally, looking as if she probably had something to do with the Battle of Bunker Hill. She didn't, of course, for the simple fact that she didn't exist during the American Revolution.

Helen, history buff, always looked as hard as being behind the wheel would allow at both Bunker Hill to her right and "Old Ironsides" to her left as she drove the bridge spanning the Mystic River.

This evening, however, her thoughts were on finding the Sullivan and Conlin Funeral Home and then deciding what she would do after that.

She was dressed in light slacks and a blouse appropriate to the solemnity of such a sad mission. Her handbag had the additional heft of her .38 Colt service revolver. Best to mix sorrow with prudence.

At the foot of the bridge, she took the cut off to Charlestown, asked a cop in a police cruiser the whereabouts of the funeral home, and drove to it.

She parked as close to it as she could and assessed the situation. Her immediate goal was to get Angelo Nolan's address and proceed from there to find out whatever she could about him.

She checked her watch. It was 8:30. The wake was seven to nine. Her strategy was to go inside so that she could identify the family and then follow them home to get Angelo Nolan's address or, more likely, his former address.

As she walked across the street, she hoped Angelo Nolan's two anthropoid friends weren't inside mourning. That could present a messy scene.

A doorman held the door for her and she stepped into a large cluster of people spilling into the hallway that led to the viewing rooms. The sign above the first room to her right said, Mrs. Collins. In the room to her left, a Mr. Brady rested. Charlestown had its share of Irish. There were two more rooms at the end of the hall.

Tentatively, she peeked into the room labeled Mr. Nolan.

Standing near the casket were two women and a teenaged boy. A handful of people was seated about the room. There was no line to view the deceased or the coffin, actually, since the casket was closed. She didn't see Kyle Peterson or Thomas Crawford but there was a smoking room to the rear and she could hear people talking in it.

The two women looked over at her inquiringly. Helen smiled and signed the book with the name of a friend who had moved to Minneapolis.

She shook the hand of the teenaged boy who had to be Angelo's younger brother and mumbled something about how sorry she was. He bobbed his head in the uncertain awkwardness of adolescence. She actually felt sorry for him.

The first and younger of the two women, mid-twenties, she took to be Angelo's sister. She, like the boy and the older woman, all strongly resembled Angelo. All of them looked Irish.

She shook the young woman's hand. "Hello, I'm Susan Jameson. I was a friend of Angelo's."

The woman nodded and smiled. "Thank you for coming. I'm Dee, Angie's sister. I don't remember Angie mentioning your name."

"We were casual friends," Helen said, feeling guilty about the whole charade.

"Mum," the woman said, turning to her mother, "this a friend of Angelo's. Susan Jameson."

Helen moved to her and shook her hand. "I'm terribly sorry, Mrs. Nolan."

"It's Marselli now." Mrs. Marselli looked at Helen sadly. Her eyes were red-rimmed. The timbre of her voice and the wrinkles that puckered her mouth were giveaways of a heavy smoker. Helen felt that smoking probably wasn't her only vice. Despite the haggardness of sorrow and none too clean lifestyle, Mrs. Marselli appeared to Helen to be in her early forties. Having had children so young probably hadn't helped either.

"Oh, I didn't know," Helen said.

Mrs. Marselli held onto Helen's hand. "You were a friend of Angelo's?"

"Yes."

"From the old neighborhood?"

"Uh, from the North Shore. I really hadn't known him all that long."

Mrs. Marselli's face clouded. "The North Shore. What the hell was he doing up there?" She seemed to ponder that a moment.

"Angelo wasn't a saint, I know that, but he was a good boy."

Mrs. Marselli clung to Helen's hand as though she didn't want to let go. She worked a smile. "Did you belong to the church?"

"Excuse me?"

"I'm sorry, I was just wondering whether you belonged to that church on the North Shore that Angelo started to go to. If that's where you met him. It was in Salem."

Helen felt her pulse pick up a bit. "Oh, yes, he mentioned something about that. He seemed to have enjoyed it very much."

"I'm trying to think of the minister's name."

This was too easy, Helen thought, but sometimes things can work out. She took a stab. "Reverend Whittaker, you mean?"

Mrs. Marselli smiled. "Yes, that was it. Angelo mentioned him. He found him an inspiration, I guess."

My, my, Helen was thinking. "Reverend Whittaker was an inspirational man."

"Was?"

"Yes. He died."

"Oh, I didn't know. Angelo never mentioned that. Recently?"

"Yes."

"Oh." Mrs. Marselli seemed to have come to a conversational dead-end. She pumped Helen's hand some more and then released it. "Well, thank you so much for coming."

Helen knelt at the casket breathing the garden smell of the flowers. There were just two arrangements: Son and Brother.

She got up just as Kyle Peterson and Thomas Crawford came into the room.

The Reverend Jan Reuter swung the hinged painting to reveal the wall safe. The painting was an original oil of surf pounding a rocky coastline done by a Stone Harbor artist who had given it to the church.

He twirled the dial, opened the safe, and took out a waxed envelope. He sat down across from Paul Clarke in an expensive stuffed chair. A brass lamp lit the room dimly, augmented a bit by light from the streetlight outside.

From the envelope, Jan Reuter took a single page of paper, parchment, actually, and skimmed the hand-written script, reading parts aloud to Paul Clarke. Paul Clarke nodded occasionally. Both he and Jan Reuter were very familiar with the contents of the letter. The reading wasn't for information so much as for confirmation that the direction they were headed was indeed the only direction.

They dug by the light of two lanterns. They had picked this night because the moon, nothing more than a slender sickle, was covered by clouds that were leaking a thin rain, not much more than a mist. The night was cold, winter would soon be here, but the six men digging were perspiring from their exertions and their anxiety.

Besides the six digging, two stood on alert with loaded muskets, and one, the leader, alternated between digging, directing, and speaking words of encouragement.

At the foot of the hill, where the river curved in and then swept out to the harbor, bobbed two longboats tied to some shrubbery.

After they had dug for perhaps fifteen minutes with the leader urging them to be careful, one man, a burly fellow, muscles and hands hardened from years aloft at sea, said to the leader, "Philip, here. I've uncovered one."

All of them, the leader, the other diggers, those guarding with muskets, quietly, almost reverently, peered down at where the man was gently brushing the earth away from a human skull.

"Here, lads, let's work together on this," Philip English said. "John and

Daniel, you bring the canvas over here."

They spread ship's canvas beside the unearthed skull and continued their careful exhumation until the rest of the skeleton, shreds of rotted clothing still clinging here and there, was uncovered.

Carefully, keeping it intact, they placed the skeleton on the canvas.

After that, the work went more quickly. When they were satisfied they had uncovered all they were going to, seventeen skeletons, one skull-less, Philip English said, "I think we have them all, lads. I had always heard that Samuel Nurse came for his mother the night of her execution and brought her back to Salem Village. Who else might not be here I do not know. But from the traces of her clothing that still be clinging to her sorry bones, I would think that this last one be Bridget Bishop. She was the first to die so she would be the last one uncovered."

The group of men gathered around the skeletons they had arranged into three mounds on three pieces of ship's canvas.

Philip English's eyes misted as he looked at them. "May God grant them peace."

"Amen," resonated from several bowed heads.

Then Philip English looked beyond the heads of his men, all who had sailed with him, all faithful to him. He looked to the north, toward Salem Village and then to the east, toward Salem Town. A string of oaths tumbled unchecked from his lips such as his friends were unaccustomed to hear him utter. "Blind, stupid," were the only words they would have repeated and these were men who sailed and whose language was as salty as the seas they sailed.

"All right, lads, let's get them onto the longboats. The tide's with us and we'll have them in Stone Harbor and in a decent Christian resting place before the sun is up."

A week later, Philip English sat in his newly built church in Stone Harbor. The church sat directly across from the sea, which now was the only continuity to his former years. His wife was dead, his fortune gone, and his health and well-being ruined. All he had was an abiding hatred for Salem and its puritans who had ruined him and taken the lives of innocents with their blind stupidity.

But he had done some final good. He had given the bones and souls of those innocents a final resting place that must remain a secret lest those same puritans come to defile them still further. He was confident the bones would never be uncovered. True, they were not buried in the earth but he had dared not do that. Eyes were everywhere. They would rest in this church. Exactly where would remain a secret that would die with him and those good lads who had helped bring those souls to this decent place. He could trust those lads. At sea, he had trusted them and they had trusted him.

Those who followed him at this church he would trust to preserve and guard the knowledge that somewhere in the church or in its land rested those victims of puritan blindness and hatred.

He dipped the quill into the pot of ink and finished the covenant he would *leave that, with God's help, would ensure those souls eternal rest.*

When he had finished, he stared thoughtfully a moment at the flickering fire in his fireplace and savored its warmth. It seemed as though years at sea had given him a chill that grew deeper and stronger as time went on, that made him live in an enduring winter.

He spread sand over the ink, let it dry a moment, and then carefully brushed the sand away.

He sat back and read what he had written.

When he had finished, Jan Reuter rested the letter on his knee and regarded Paul Clarke. "We must never forget that we're not alone on this thing, Paul. It's really a sacred trust handed down and handed down."

Paul Clarke nodded in agreement. "But why did the trouble have to come on your watch? I mean, after all these years."

Jan Reuter shrugged but smiled in appreciation of the other man's understanding.

"And I must say that you've handled it admirably."

"Well, that remains to be seen," Jan Reuter said. "You know, the part that gets me is that this . . ." He waved the letter. "Is that this is misleading. The way it's worded you'd think they had been buried outside. If I had know, I'd never have let that fool Lincoln Southwick work on the foundation."

"Yes, I agree. It is misleading. Perhaps done deliberately as a safeguard?"

"Perhaps."

They sat quietly a moment. The night was very chilly and the air damp from an off-shore breeze. Paul Clarke had lit a fire in the fireplace, the season's first, and the wood snapped quietly as it burned.

"How are things proceeding on your end?" Jan Reuter asked.

"We should have what we need by the end of the week. As you can imagine, it's not an easy item to come by."

"I should imagine it isn't. And the source will be discreet?"

Paul Clarke nodded. "Absolutely."

"How much did you have to tell him?"

"Well, that was a problem. At first, I tried to tell him nothing but found I was getting nowhere. You'll have to admit that it's a very unusual request."

Jan Reuter allowed himself a smile. "I'll concede that." Then the smile evaporated as he anticipated he was about to hear something he wouldn't like.

"In the end I had to tell him. There was no other way."

"Everything?"

"Well, a lot of it is out anyway. I mean what with television and the papers it's not as though he hadn't heard of the skeletons at all."

Jan Reuter sighed. "I suppose so." Absently, he tapped the parchment on his knee.

"By the way," he said, "I've been working on my end. I'll be flying to London Monday morning. And I'll be back Thursday evening. That should be plenty of time."

Paul Clarke leaned forward eagerly. "What did he say?"

"Well, naturally, I didn't go into any kind of detail on the phone. But I made it unmistakably clear that we were dealing with a crisis here and I had to talk with him. I had to have his . . . his input."

Jan Reuter despised using a word like 'input' but couldn't think quickly of a synonym. He hated new words of that ilk: input, feedback, network. The jargon of a culture losing its feel for words of richness and texture.

He got up and returned the letter, in its waxed envelope, to the safe. He sat back down and smiled bleakly at Paul Clarke. "So," he said, "by this time next week we should be well on our way to containing all of this and permanently shutting up the meddlesome Mr. Sennot and Ms. Helen Waters."

Kyle Peterson and Thomas Crawford sat next to a young woman who seemed to be by herself and engaged her in hushed conversation. Helen averted her gaze, turning her face to her left and smiling at Mrs. Marselli and Angelo Nolan's siblings. Feeling foolish, she kept her head turned as she walked from the room. On the sidewalk, she looked back but no one was behind her.

In her truck, she sat and waited and watched. It was ten to nine. She opened her purse and checked the .38 and then chided herself for nervousness.

The revelation about The Reverend Fred Whittaker had been interesting indeed and she puzzled over it. She'd like to run it by Mike Doyle but now she wondered whether she could ever run anything by him again. Talk about not knowing your friends.

Just before nine, the funeral home emptied, a stream of people hitting the sidewalk, most from the Collins and Brady wakes, some pausing to chat a moment. Peterson and Crawford were among the last to leave.

Shortly after nine, the families came out. Helen watched Mrs. Marselli and Angelo's brother and sister walk to an old Plymouth Reliant in the funeral home parking lot. When the Reliant pulled out, she followed.

Charlestown isn't very big and they traveled only a few blocks before the Reliant parked in front of a brick duplex.

Helen kept going and stopped at the next intersection. Fortunately, no cars were behind her and she could linger long enough to see Angelo Nolan's family go into the duplex.

That was what she wanted. An address. She took note of the names of the intersecting streets and pulled away.

She had told Joe she'd meet him at Lily's in Quincy Market at 9:30.

The next day was gray and cold. In the pre-dawn dark, Helen dressed for her morning's work. Heavy sweats and a hat today, the garb of early November. She had a long day. The *Working Girl* this morning and back to Charlestown this afternoon.

She made oatmeal in the microwave, feeling that she might as well get into the whole chilly weather thing, and brewed two cups of coffee. An English muffin and a glass of orange juice completed her breakfast.

Her grandmother was still sleeping, as she usually was when Helen prepared for her workday. She clicked on the small counter TV and turned the volume way down. She always watched the early morning news before she went out on the water. The weather was especially important.

Her father had done the same thing. "When you're out on the ocean, the weather's a lot more than just small talk," he used to tell her. "You gotta be careful. You never take anything for granted. Like with guns."

All the caution, though, hadn't prepared him for the sudden squall that took his life. Every time she went out, Helen lived with that memory of him and that possibility for herself.

Except for three years when she was a cop and shared an apartment in Salem, this was the home she had known all her life.

She grew up here, went to school from here, and returned after her father had died. Her mother had been dead for two years before the sea took her father and Helen couldn't bear the thought of her grandmother being alone with haunting memories in the home she had lived in with her son, daughter-in-law and granddaughter.

She ate some oatmeal, dotted with plump, swollen raisins, and sweetened with honey. Helen had come back so that her grandmother wouldn't be alone with haunting memories. And she wasn't. Helen shared them with her. The ghosts of her parents visited her every day from the mantel pictures that froze them at points in their lives, from their wedding day to later days. In some, Helen smiled between them, her father's arm draped across her shoulder, her mother's hand atop her head.

Sometimes, less often than she used to, she would still go into her parents' room, kept as it had been. It was the room she supposed she had been conceived in, the room where she slept between them when she was a little girl, fevered and achy, or fearful from the demons of childhood dreams.

She thought about what she had done last night, what she had been doing the last two or three days. Going into rooms where she had no business. That's what Mike Doyle had been telling her, not in so many words, but his meaning had been unmistakably clear.

But Mike Doyle didn't matter any more except as an official presence who, as such, couldn't altogether be ignored.

Her father had been a great cop, a believer in the worth of what he did. In the eulogy to her father, the Chief had said that John Waters believed in and practiced the sanctity of the law. Helen knew those weren't mere words said just to say something nice about the dead.

"You can't look away, Helen, when the bad guys are doing their dirt. As a cop, you sure can't and even an ordinary person can't. The problem is that too many do. And when ordinary people look away that makes our job even harder."

She knew that's why she wasn't looking away now. It wasn't just because she and Joe were in the church when Angelo Nolan and his friends tried to burn it down. Her father used to say that just because the bad guys weren't aiming at you doesn't mean you pretend they aren't there.

The weather person, a smiling curly-haired young man, had finished making inane chitchat with the anchor and was giving his forecast. Cloudy skies, chilly temps for this time of year, chance of showers, winds out of the northeast. Seas choppy.

Definitely a day to be careful.

By 10:30 she was back out of the water with not much to show for an abbreviated morning's work besides a bad case of nerves. The wind had picked up a lot with gusts up to 50 knots and swells that sent any prudent sailor packing. A thin rain mixed with the salt spray.

No one was at the wharf and she had a hard time tying the *Working Girl* up. When she climbed up, Charlie Goodwin came out of his shack hunched over in yellow rain slicker.

"You just comin' in, Helen? This is no day to be out. You should know better."

"Wasn't like this when I left, Charlie. Got a little meaner out there than they predicted."

"Did you bring in anything?"

"Just myself."

Charlie squinted into the wind-driven spray and rain. "Just in time, I'd say. I think there are still a few out. Haven't heard any distress signals but I'll keep listening."

At home, Mabel already had a fire dancing to the tune of the wind in the fireplace chimney. When Helen came out of her hot bath in a large blue cotton robe and was toweling her hair, her grandmother inquired about the previous evening. For a moment, Helen was taken back until she realized the question pertained to how things were going with Joe.

She knew her grandmother was anxious for her to settle down as a nicely domesticated housewife, sewing, darning, and cooking, and that she saw Joe as the man she should do that with. She conceded that it wasn't an altogether unattractive image although she doubted she could take too much of sitting still by the hearthside knitting and planning the next meal.

Mabel looked at her granddaughter carefully. "You shouldn't have gone out, today."

"It wasn't that bad when I left. I came right in when it picked up. Don't worry, I'm careful."

"So was your father."

"Gram, there's risk in everything." She went to her grandmother and kissed her forehead. "But I am careful. I really am. What are you reading?"

"Oh, nothing." Mabel Waters put the book she had been reading on her lap, the cover down.

"Is that a book on witchcraft? God, there's no escaping it, is there?"

Reluctantly, it seemed to Helen, her grandmother held up the book. "It's just silly nonsense. Something to pass the time."

Helen examined the cover. "Hmmm. What's it about? Medicines, potions, that kind of thing?"

"I told you it was just nonsense."

"It is. I'm surprised at you."

"Something to pass the time," Mabel repeated. "It's harmless."

"Gram, I'm going into Boston for a while."

"Oh, to see Joe?"

"Well, yeah, later probably. I'm, uh, going to do a little shopping first."

"So you won't be home for supper?"

"I don't know. You go ahead and I'll get for myself if I'm home."

Mabel Waters smiled and patted her granddaughter's hand.

"You have a good time, Dear. Say hi to Joe. Invite him back for a meal soon. Now that his work at the church is over we don't want him becoming a stranger."

Mabel Waters watched her granddaughter walk to her room to dress and then with a contented smile turned back to her book on the various potions of Wicca. Nonsense indeed.

She started at a variety store just around the corner and down the street from the house where Angelo Nolan's family lived. She wondered whether this was a fool's mission, trying to dig up information about a dead man in this neighborhood. Charlestown, a lily-white neighborhood, had a notorious code of silence about the murders (white on white) committed there. It had even been the subject of national television a couple of times. Maybe the code extended to keeping silent about one of its denizens with a none too savory past.

The store was a Mom and Pop and Pop was at the helm when Helen walked in. Two teenage boys from the current mold were buying lunch, a couple of bags of Doritos and two large bottles of Pepsi. They had baseball hats on backwards, baggy pants with crotches hanging to the knees, and shirts that could serve as tents in a pinch. Helen waited for them to leave before she went to the counter.

"Hi, how're you doing?" she said.

The man smiled, the automatic response to a damn good-looking woman. "I'm fine. How are you doing today?"

Helen beamed back. "Kind of a lousy day but I'm doing great. Look, I'm wondering if you can help me out. I'm trying to do a follow up on the Nolan kid who died a couple of days ago up in Salem. Did you know him?"

The man's smile snapped shut and his look became guarded, head lowered a bit and gaze averted like a dog warily approaching a stranger. He appeared late fifties, gray hair—a full head—parted neatly, average height, a bit overweight but not off the charts. He wore outdated horn-rimmed glasses.

"A follow up?"

"Yeah, I'm free lance and I thought it might be an interesting story. You know, kid from the big city goes to the North Shore. Gets friendly with a minister up there, the church and so on, and dies." Helen lowered her voice. "Maybe suspiciously."

The man nodded but didn't say anything.

"So I'm just trying to get a little background about Angelo."

The man regarded Helen evenly and she felt her gaze start to break. This was stupid. The ploy about being a free-lance reporter was idiotic, she felt, something out of dozens of novels.

"What did you say your name was?"

"Helen Waters." She had to go with the real name in case he asked for identification. Hell, she could be starting a career as a free-lance reporter.

"Well, Helen, I'll tell you something. I know you're not supposed to speak badly about the dead but Angelo Nolan was a no good son of a bitch. I'm surprised he didn't get it a long time ago. By the way, you didn't get it from me."

"Of course not."

The man wiped at something on the counter with his hand. Behind him, were rows of lottery scratch cards hanging in rolls.

"Uh, is there anything in particular that makes you say that?"

"Hell, yes. A lot of things. But . . . " The man waved his hand as though he had said enough.

Helen fished in her mind for a question that would keep the well flowing.

"You know who I feel bad for?" the man said. "I feel bad for his mother. She's a nice lady and she's had a real tough time of it with that jerk."

"Could—"

"Look." The man leaned across the counter. "Tell you what. Go to the *Herald*. You know Gerland Hahn who writes a column there? Caustic bastard for my money but tells it like it is. He knows everything that's going on in Charlestown. You talk to him. You're a reporter. He'll tell you stuff make your ears bleed."

Helen nodded. "Thanks."

"Don't thank me, Helen. I didn't tell you a goddam thing."

A gust of wind shook the door and windows to the store. The rain had picked up and slapped against the glass.

"Stay dry," the man said and turned his attention to some sheets of paper by the cash register.

Gerland Hahn had a daunting reputation. He wrote gritty street stories and was a real hard line, way to the right kind of guy. Helen had read his column a few times but his black/white, right/wrong view of things and his acerb style turned her off.

She couldn't picture herself confronting him (if he'd agree to see her) with her free-lance reporter pose. He'd see through that very quickly. She was surprised the guy in the store hadn't. She had been prepared for a complete stone wall. "Sorry, lady, don't know any Angelo Nolan. See you later." The guy had been cautious but he had spilled a little.

She'd heard Gerland Hahn was a womanizer, by no means an unusual category it seemed for a man to belong to. From politicians to priests, men were in eternal rut for anything that reeked of estrogen. Her father hadn't been that way.

Maybe she ought to change into something slinky, show him a bit of thigh, a smidgen of cleavage, and a hint that there was a lot more that could come his way. All he had to do was share a few insights about Angelo Nolan (the no good son of a bitch) and she'd be mighty grateful indeed.

She laughed as she thought of herself as a femme fatale and knew that she'd probably laugh at herself while trying to carry it off and thereby ruin the whole ploy.

She started the truck and let the engine idle a moment. The windshield wipers left smears and streaks and she had to peer strategically to see clearly.

No, there had to be another way to approach Gerland Hahn and she thought she knew what it might be. She glanced up at the Bunker Hill Monument looming not far away and headed back to Stone Harbor. She'd find a gas station on the way and get some new wiper blades.

Before heading home, she stopped at the Salem *Star* building. The *Star*, Salem's daily newspaper, had recently moved its operation to a new location in a refurbished warehouse on the waterfront of what had once been the South River but which long ago had been filled in to the extent that it now was a narrow, straight channel. Still, it was water and pleasure boats sailed back and forth and everyone seemed to think it was a spiffy new location.

She sat in the office of Leroy Geratowski, a reporter she had befriended when she was a cop. They used to exchange scuttlebutt and had been the source, unofficially, of information to one another.

Leroy Geratowski, whom everyone called Gerry, was smoking his fourth cigarette of the day in a tapering down program that included lots of chewing gum, biofeedback, and gnawed fingernails.

"You look great, Helen. The seafaring life agrees with you apparently."

"I like it, Gerry. But it's not an easy living. And it's getting tougher and tougher."

"Tell me. Every day, it seems, we get a story about the plight of the fisherman. So, what brings you by? Price gouging on lobster by some of the restaurants? It's been going on, I hear."

She smiled. "Still fighting the weed, huh?"

"Those cigarette company CEOs ought to be strung up. But I shall fight the good fight and in the end I will prevail." He snuffed out his cigarette and leaned back, his hands behind his head. He was close to forty, undisciplined sparse hair going in pretty much whatever direction it wanted, thin of limb and shoulder, but too much fast food and beer showing in a slight but definite paunch.

"Gerry, how well do you know Gerland Hahn?"

He leaned forward and smiled broadly, revealing a lot of dental work and the need for more. "Gerland Hahn!" He thrust his right arm straight out. "Heil Hitler! So, Fraulein, vat do you vant vis Herr Hahn?"

Helen laughed and went along. "None of your business, you svine. I simply vant to talk vis him."

Leroy Geratowski leaned back again, still smiling. "Well, I'll say this. You should at least get out alive. You're obviously Arian. No sign of latent genes of, how should I put it? Oh let's be honest about it, no signs of inferior races. You know, Mediterranean types, or, heaven forbid, Spanish-speaking types or African heritage. Your features display no Semitic stock and you don't have the look of a daughter of Lesbos. Far from it, I might say." He raised his hand palm out. "Not that I have anything against lesbians. Yeah, you'd survive a conversation with old Gerland. 'Course, he'd probably warp your mind."

Leroy Geratowski went to his pack of Marlboro Lights. "See what you've made me do? Just thinking about that direct descendant of Attila raises my blood pressure."

He lit up and inhaled deeply as though he were breathing in the airs of paradise. "Now, seriously, may I be so bold as to inquire why a nice young lady like you would want anything to do with that Gestapo wannabe?"

"You, heard, I assume, about the young man who died the other night after leaving the Wet Spot? Angelo Nolan?"

"Sure did. Christ, was he connected to Gerland? I mean, he was pretty far to the right himself. Probably not so much as an ideology, the way it is with Gerland, although he'd deny it, but just as a justification for violence and general hate."

"Whoa. How much do you know about Nolan?" Maybe there would be no need to talk with Gerland Hahn.

"Not much. Just hearsay. You know. Talk." Gerry took another deep drag, turned his head and blew the smoke away from Helen. "You know, we're not even supposed to be smoking in this building at all? Only the fact that I have my own office, such as it is, lets me get away with it."

"Things are tough all around, Gerry. So, come on. What have you heard about Angelo Nolan?"

"I guess the logical thing for me to ask is, why do you want to know?"

Briefly, she told him about the attempted torching of the church in Stone Harbor and her subsequent conversation with Mike Doyle after the death of Angelo Nolan.

When she had finished, Gerry took a final drag and snuffed out his cigarette with ferocity. "Sounds like murky waters, Helen. But Doyle doesn't have a thing as far as you're concerned. Does he?"

"Of course not."

"Only kidding. I thought he was your buddy. Former partners and all that."

"Blows my mind, I'll tell you. I don't know what he's doing rattling my cage like that."

"Well, I can tell you a little about Angelo Nolan. But it's all street talk, you understand. Hey, you want a coffee or anything?"

Helen shook her head.

"First, Nolan's death is definitely a homicide. That's not street talk, really, but it's unofficial at this point. Poison is the probable cause of death. Cops'll be making an announcement soon. By the way, what I'm hearing is that it's the same stuff that did in the Reverend Fred Whittaker."

"Doesn't surprise me," Helen said.

"Tell me you didn't know about a connection between Whittaker and Nolan."

"Afraid I can't tell you that, Gerry. But I don't know any more than that. I mean, I don't know the nature of that relationship."

"It wasn't holy, I can tell you that much."

Gerry picked up a pack of gum from his desk and proffered a piece to Helen who declined. He unwrapped a stick and popped it into his mouth.

"I'm not exactly sure myself what their connection was," he said, "except that I hear Angelo went a visiting the Reverend's digs from time to time. Now, I could be wrong, but I don't think the Reverend Fred was any Father Flanagan."

Gerry chomped on his gum a moment as if reflecting on its properties. "You know what's kind of strange? After Whittaker died, Angelo and his friends, who, by the way, as far as I know, never visited Whittaker, wore black armbands."

"Maybe then they had some kind of genuinely good relationship with him."

"Maybe. You mean the Father Flanagan type routine. I doubt it. These are the kinds of guys who go in big for the symbols of things. You know, like right wing patriots who get all bent about flag burning but couldn't give two shits about the plight of certain kinds of people in the country the flag represents. Whittaker dies so they wear armbands. Wearing the bands elevates him and thereby somehow justifies any kinds of nefarious activities they may have been involved in with him."

"Like what?"

Gerry shrugged.

"Come on, Gerry, for crying out loud. You don't come up with a theory like that based on just a hunch."

"Why not? Angelo and his buddies are trouble. In and out of scrapes with the Boston cops. Never did any time, apparently, but not 4-H-ers. Plus, there's Whittaker himself."

Gerry let the statement hang.

"Yeah," Helen prodded after a moment, "what about him?"

"Well, I don't really know for sure except, of course, why would he have anything to do with those guys?"

"We're talking in circles."

"And . . . "

"And?" Helen said.

"And, it seems, the Reverend was a bit of a womanizer."

"Oh, hell. Another icon topples. I mean, yeah, not exemplary behavior in a man of the cloth but so what? Don't tell me that shocks you. I wouldn't be surprised to learn the Pope has a harem."

"Hey, Helen, you came to me, remember? I'm just telling you what I know—which, admittedly, ain't much—and what I think."

"You're right. Sorry."

"Besides . . ."

"Go ahead."

"Nothing. Forget it."

"Gerry, I'm sorry, I didn't mean to sound unappreciative. Tell me. I promise I won't sneer."

"It's nothing. Forget it."

Helen nodded. "Okay. Look, I really do appreciate your talking with me."

"What the hell are you going to do with all this?"

"That's the question, isn't it?"

They sat through a moment's pause, Gerry chewing and enjoying looking at Helen and Helen pensively biting gently at a fingernail.

She stood and extended her hand. "Thank you, Gerry."

"Sure. Hey, look, some free advice, Helen. You're not a cop anymore. Enjoy the ocean, enjoy your fishing. Forget all this crap. Let the cops who get paid to handle this stuff do just that."

Helen smiled. "Maybe that's the point, Gerry."

Chapter Fifteen

The woman with the classic profile sat and considered ways and means. She sipped herbal tea and debated with herself the most effective way to kill Helen Waters.

The tea was excellent, not at all like the horrid stuff the Reverend Fred Whittaker had been wont to serve her before they made love. How could a man so otherwise refined and intelligent have such plebeian tastes? Well, in his defense, he certainly wasn't the first or the only person in the world who thought tea was bought in supermarkets and had to be doctored with milk and sugar.

Killing Helen Waters the way she had killed Fred Whittaker and Angelo Nolan had a lot to recommend it. It was quick, it was effective, and by no means was it messy. Guns (which she didn't understand anyway and certainly were messy), knives (also messy and requiring dexterity and surprise), baseball bats whacking skulls (messy), and shoves from balconies (messy— although the mess should be distant—and requiring a balcony and positioning of person to be pushed) couldn't match the pinch or two of powder mixed into a drink.

The problem, as she saw it, was that, if a third person were to succumb by the same rather exotic means, the police would really start to concentrate and focus. Not that she felt particularly intimidated by their abilities but prudence was one of her stronger qualities.

On the other hand, this was to be the last. With Helen Waters out of the way, that should end the need for such terminations. Of course, one never knew.

She certainly didn't see herself as some kind of serial killer. She wasn't one of those pathetic little men you saw on the television news being led away by the police, trying to hide their face from the camera, after having killed scads of people, maybe performing grisly rituals on them or even eating them and then burying whatever remained in their basement or back yard. She wasn't deranged. Full moons didn't trigger her nor did unexplained compulsions induced by something sinister and dark from her childhood that she had driven deep into her subconscious.

No. She had behaved pragmatically. Her motives had been pragmatic, nothing more, nothing less.

And so it would be with Helen Waters. She must be eliminated and it was best done soon. If the deed must be done, best to do it quickly. Didn't Shakespeare say something like that? In her mind, she went through the plays. *Macbeth*, maybe. Perhaps *Caesar*. She wasn't sure. She'd have to check when she had a chance. The man had a way with words. Something for every occasion.

So, it was settled. At least the means. Helen would take a little drink and that would be it. Sweet dreams.

The question now, beyond soon, was exactly when. It wouldn't do to be passive on this and simply wait for the opportunity to present itself.

The woman with the classic profile sipped her tea and thought of ways to force the moment.

After talking with Leroy Geratowski, Helen had called Gerland Hahn's extension at the *Herald* but got his answering machine and decided not to leave a message. That was yesterday. She tried again this morning with the same results. The rain had stopped but the wind was still more than brisk and the seas were still too rough. She'd try Gerland Hahn's number again later.

She decided she'd spend the morning in Salem trying to learn whatever she could about the Reverend Fred Whittaker. She breakfasted on cereal, a bagel, juice, and coffee. She put on tan slacks, a black blouse, and grabbed a light jacket. After checking on her still-sleeping grandmother again, she went out to her truck. As always, whenever she was dressed in anything but work clothes and wasn't headed toward the wharf, she wished she were driving something else. Something with flair. Something with curvy lines and a stylish spoiler behind the passengers' seat rather than a dented and rusted eight-foot metal bed with a tailgate that was becoming more and more obstinate.

She started at the Salem Public Library, and found that Mary Rose would be in shortly. She got all the issues of the Salem *Star*, beginning with the day following the Reverend Fred Whittaker's death. She read through everything that had to do with Whittaker's death or about the man himself. When she finished, she felt she knew nothing more than what she had already known, namely that the Reverend Fred Whittaker, respected pastor of the First Congregational Church of Salem, had been the victim of foul play. The post mortem revealed that cause of death had been ingestion of a toxic substance. None of the articles revealed what that toxic substance might be.

The biographical information about the Reverend revealed that originally he was from Iowa, although his ancestral roots were in Salem; that he had served at the First Congregational for fourteen years; that he was 48 years old and had been a widower for almost five years.

Everything about Fred Whittaker seemed exemplary yet both Mike Doyle and Leroy Geratowski had hinted very strongly that Fred Whittaker had led less than an exemplary life.

She returned the newspapers and went out to her truck. The fallish air was crisp and clear, football and apple feeling. Bands of small white clouds scurried across a sharp blue sky.

She started her truck and headed for the First Congregational Church, which was less than five minutes away.

The man had called Paul Clarke the night before and said he had been able to get the item sooner than he anticipated. Now he was at the rectory door beaming at Paul Clarke as he held up the cardboard box about big enough to hold a basketball.

Paul Clarke beamed back. "Come in," he said. When the bell had rung, he rushed to the door ahead of the housekeeper, Jenny Perkins. He beckoned his visitor to a seat in the living room and sat across from him.

"So," he said, when he was certain Jenny had safely retreated, "you got it." He nodded at the cardboard box, a plain brown thing that looked as if it had originally held drinking glasses or something similar.

"Yes. It should do very well, I would think, based on what you told me. Would you care to see it?" The man held the box on his lap. He was a short man, probably late fifties, with fully developed male-pattern baldness leaving only the classic ring of hair around the sides and back of the head. He was dressed in chino work shirt and work pants. He wore ankle-high work boots.

"I suppose I should."

"Is Dr. Reuter here? He'll want a look too, I should imagine."

"He's out of town. London, actually," Paul Clarke said importantly. "But I'm authorized to make a judgement, not that I've got any expertise on these things. What it comes down to, I guess, is that I've got to trust your judgement."

The man smiled. "What's to judge, what's to trust? It's male and it's two-hundred and seventy-five years old. Close enough, I should think, that no kind of testing is going to be able to say it's not quite old enough."

Paul Clarke nodded. "Uh, if you don't mind, just how did you get it? I mean, I know in general but, well, you know . . ."

His voice trailed.

The man grinned, revealing the perfect smile of false teeth.

"I did everything myself when no one else was around. I used the backhoe, did the digging, opened the old pine box—it was still in pretty good shape, believe it or not—reached in and pulled it out. I mean it was in a section no one ever goes to anymore. Even the other workers. It's overgrown and there sure 'n shit aren't going to be any relatives or friends coming by "

He looked at Paul Clarke carefully, enjoying the wince he had caught at the 'sure 'n shit.'

"But, here, check it out." He started to hold the box out to Paul Clarke and then pulled it back. "First, though, I think, you know . . . "

Paul Clarke stared blankly a moment.

"You know what we said. Cash. I mean, it's got to be cash. There's no other way."

"Of course." Paul Clarke reached inside his jacket and pulled out a white envelope, which he handed to the man.

The man opened it and smiled. "That's the beauty of big bills, isn't it. Makes counting easy."

He handed the box on his lap to Paul Clarke who opened it and looked in at the human skull staring back at him.

For a few moments, Helen sat across from the church and regarded it closely. She had, of course, seen it many times before both as a police officer driving by in her cruiser and, before and after that, as an ordinary citizen. But she had never paid it any particular attention.

The church was fieldstone and looked Old World, like something that belonged in England, Wales, or Scotland, she thought. A high wrought-iron fence set it off from the brick sidewalk. Three sugar maples, tall and gnarled with age, towered in front of it. Already they showed patches of autumn blaze.

She walked across and paused by the crushed stone walkway that led to the minister's house. A glass-encased sign with removable letters read, THIS IS NONE OTHER BUT THE HOUSE OF GOD, AND THIS IS THE GATE OF HEAVEN. Genesis 17

She knew she should turn back to her truck. She had, quite literally, no business here. She wasn't a police officer any more. She wasn't a private detective. She thought of the free-lance reporter ruse and decided maybe it wasn't so bad after all.

She had a pen and pad in her shoulder bag. She could be doing an article. So what if she was unable to sell it? Beyond all that, she recognized the futility of trying to find anything that the cops hadn't found. Then she thought of Mike Doyle and her feelings of disquiet about him and the entire matter.

She walked up the stone walkway and pushed the button by the door which produced an ordinary ring, just a harsh electric buzz, actually. She had expected something deep-toned and sonorous, something in keeping with the look of Britain and fieldstone, with THE HOUSE OF GOD and THE GATE OF HEAVEN.

She waited and pressed again almost hoping for no answer to justify just walking back to her truck and driving back to Stone Harbor. She thought of what Leroy Geratowski had said. "Enjoy the ocean, enjoy your fishing. Forget all this crap."

The door opened. A plump, pleasant woman, steel-gray hair pulled back in a bun, rimless glasses bouncing sunlight at Helen, smiled at her.

"Good morning," she said.

"Good morning. And isn't it a lovely day? My name is Helen Waters and I'm a free-lance writer. Uh, this may seem intrusive and inappropriate—and please don't hesitate to tell me if it is—but I'd like very much to do a profile of Reverend Whittaker. I understand he was a wonderful man and I'd hate to see him ultimately remembered mainly as just another of today's so many murder victims."

The words 'God, woman, have you no shame,' ran through her mind in involuntary self-admonishment.

The pleasant woman's smile faded but her head nodded in agreement with something Helen had said.

"I was wondering," Helen said, "if there was someone here who could talk with me a bit about Reverend Whittaker. Just for a few moments."

"Well, now that he's gone," the woman said, "I'm the only one here until his replacement comes in next week. That would be Reverend Johnson."

"Would you have a few moments?"

The woman hesitated. "I suppose. You're a writer, you say?"

"Yes. Free-lance."

"I'm sorry, what did you say your name is again?"

"Helen Waters."

"I wonder whether you could show me some identification."

"Well, I can show you identification that I'm Helen Waters but not that I'm a free-lance writer." She smiled. "That's what free lance is, after all. No affiliation."

"Of course. No, no, that won't be necessary," she said as Helen offered her driver's license. "Please. Come inside."

She led Helen to a comfortable living room and beckoned her to a stuffed chair. She sat on a matching sofa opposite her. "I'm Emma Wilt. I've been housekeeper here for longer than I'd like to think. Well, why be coy? Almost forty years."

Helen smiled.

"Would you care for something? Some tea maybe? Coffee?"

"Thank you, no. I really don't want to take much of your time. Just one or two questions." She took out her pad and pen.

"I guess I'm looking for things that made the man. You know, the sort of thing beyond what the newspapers carried. Beyond the obvious, the obvious being, I suppose, that he was a man of God. I mean, as a generality. But what specifically did he do? The kind of thing that makes him more than an abstraction. Beyond his congregation, I imagine most people of Salem barely knew him at all." Helen wondered whether she was fumbling this but she couldn't just come out and say, Look, I've heard that old Fred may have had a few skeletons kicking around the closet so, you know, what were they?

Emma Wilt looked at Helen steadily. "I don't know what I can tell you beyond the obvious or beyond what the newspapers said." She shrugged. "Well, he worked hard on his sermons. Spent some time writing them and practiced them aloud. His predecessor, Reverend Flagg, seldom did that. Is that the kind of thing you want?"

"Yes," Helen said, remembering to write it down.

The thing was to feed this woman things. Get her talking. See where it led, if anywhere.

"How about hobbies? Relaxation?"

"He read a lot." Helen thought she saw something in Emma Wilt's expression.

"Novels? History? The Bible, I imagine."

"Yes. All of that. He had eclectic taste. Very eclectic."

Helen smiled, sensing something here but not sure how to draw it out. She looked about. There were built in bookshelves but they had been cleared out pretty much.

"As you can see," Emma Wilt said, "I've begun to clear his things out. Starting with the bookcases. Don't know what I'll do with the books. Got them packed in boxes for now. Maybe Reverend Johnson will have a yard sale." Emma Wilt hesitated. "The problem is with some of those books you'd be awfully embarrassed selling them from a church."

Helen arched an eyebrow inquisitively. "Oh?"

"Maybe I'm old fashioned but what I'm saying is that some of Reverend Whittaker's books were not what I would have assumed a minister would read, if you know what I'm driving at. None of his predecessors read books like that."

"Do you mean, uh, smutty books?" Helen asked.

Emma Wilt responded with a tight-lipped smile and a nod. "Magazines too. But I've thrown those out. He got a lot of books from the library, too. I would think the man would have been ashamed taking them out." She looked at Helen sharply. "You won't print that, will you? I'd appreciate it if you wouldn't. I shouldn't have said anything."

"Certainly not, if that's what you wish. That will be off the record."

"Thank you."

Helen decided to try another tack and maybe come back to the reading. A man of the cloth reading dirty books and magazines certainly didn't prove anything beyond itself and probably wasn't all that uncommon, although it hinted that maybe other darker things lurked in hiding.

"I understand his wife died a few years ago. Did he socialize at all?"

"He'd have people in from time to time. Friends would call by. He'd attend church suppers, that sort of thing."

"Friends are so important then, aren't they? They can be such a comfort."

Emma Wilt started to say something but caught herself.

Helen smiled, trying to show encouragement without too much eagerness.

"I could tell you a thing or two about his friends but I think I've said quite enough."

"I'm sensing things here that I certainly didn't expect," Helen said. "Quite at variance with the persona I had heard about. I certainly didn't come here to dig dirt so perhaps it would be best if I just left "

She started to put her pad and pen away.

"And I certainly am not one to gossip, especially about the dead," Emma Wilt said. "This isn't gossip and I don't suppose it's anything you could print because I won't give you names. I can't. The police wanted names but I couldn't give them simply because I didn't know them to give. But women would visit Reverend Whittaker after his wife died."

She looked Helen in the eye, "You know what I mean by 'visit', I assume."

"I assume I do."

"Always at night and always he would answer the door before I could. I didn't know his daily comings and goings so I cannot speak of any assignations he may have had during the daylight hours."

"Why are you telling me things?" Helen asked. "Especially if you don't want me to print them."

"It bothered me. The hypocrisy. You hear about so much disgraceful behavior amongst the clergy today. In a way, I felt almost as if I were somehow embroiled in it. I guess I'm just using you as a receptacle for my feelings. Probably what I want is that you won't write anything about Reverend Whittaker. I don't want you to repeat anything I've said but I don't want some glowing eulogy about him either."

"I appreciate your being so forthright. This must not be easy for you."

"No, it certainly isn't. I'll tell you this, too. He also had some male visitors you wouldn't expect. Well, actually one. A young male visitor from time to time.

But that was more recent. I can't imagine the nature of that relationship."

"Perhaps he was simply counseling him."

"Somehow I doubt it. But I should be Christian and give him the benefit of the doubt, I suppose."

Helen was sure the young man in question was Angelo Nolan but best to be certain. She knew that if she appeared too pushy she could easily cause Emma Wilt to clam up. Cause her to wilt, she thought, almost laughing at the pun. She ventured a question. "What was there about this young man that makes you question the nature of the relationship?"

"Oh, you can tell, you know. He didn't look the type to be church going. Looked more like a hooligan of some kind. I shouldn't say this, but he certainly didn't look like a Congregationalist. If anything, he was a Papist. Looked black Irish or Italian, not that there's anything wrong with that."

Helen nodded. Emma Wilt lived in a narrow world. She wasn't sure how useful this visit had been. Fred Whittaker read dirty books and had affairs, according to Emma Wilt. So what? Maybe one of his paramours did him in.

Helen stood and extended her hand. "Thank you so much for your time, Mrs. Wilt."

"*Miss* Wilt."

"I'm disappointed I don't have a story to write but I'm disappointed to hear of another example of the frailty of a minister of God. But it's not new, I'm sure you know. Remember the *Canterbury Tales*?"

Emma Wilt snorted. "Papists."

As she made her way to the door, Helen's eyes swept the room for anything that might be revealing about the man who had lived in it. On an end table were two new library books but their titles seemed innocuous.

Helen bade Emma Wilt good day and walked to her truck past the sign that read THIS IS NONE OTHER BUT THE HOUSE OF GOD, AND THIS IS THE GATE OF HEAVEN.

She drove back to the Salem Public Library there to see if Mary Rose had gotten in yet. Sure enough, she sat at the librarian's desk hunched over a book.

"Oh, hi, Helen," she said with a cheerful smile when she looked up.

"Morning, Mary Rose. What are you reading? You seemed engrossed."

Mary Rose held up a heavy book. "Stephen King's latest. It's good, as usual. God, how does he do it? I mean, the man's so prolific."

Mary Rose looked quizzically at Helen. "What are you doing ashore? No fishing today?"

"Too rough out there, today, Mary Rose."

"Yeah, I can imagine with this wind. I don't know how you do it. I'd get sea sick on a pool float."

Helen laughed. "Mary Rose, I was wondering, could you tell what books a person had withdrawn with that computer? I mean over the course of a year, let's say." She nodded at the computer sitting on the desk in front of Mary Rose.

Mary Rose shook her head. "No. Why?"

"Nothing important. I was just curious about the titles that a certain person withdrew from the library."

"Oh?"

"It doesn't really matter anyway. The titles wouldn't reveal anything in all likelihood."

"This sounds mysterious. You've made me curious."

"It's nothing."

"Come on. You can't come in here and tantalize me like that. What are you up to?"

"It's stupid. I'd rather not say."

Mary Rose put on a pouty little girl's face. "Pretty please."

Helen rolled her eyes self deprecatingly. "Oh, all right. Remember that minister murdered in Salem?"

Mary Rose shrugged.

"The Reverend Fred Whittaker. Poisoned supposedly."

Mary Rose furrowed her brow. "Oh, yes, sure. What on earth do you want to know what books he took from the library for?"

"Mary Rose, I told you this was stupid. Just pretend I didn't even come in here, okay?"

"O-kay," Mary Rose said, smiling.

"Look," Helen said, obviously embarrassed. "Drop by some time for lobsters and chowder. Maybe I'll tell you then what this is all about."

"You're on. That's an offer I can't refuse. You've definitely got me intrigued. Even more than this Stephen King novel."

The woman with the classic profile sat and pondered. She considered and reconsidered. Not what she had to do but how she had to do it. What was established beyond any doubt was that that meddlesome bitch Helen Waters had to die. Her qualms about using poison on a third person had settled into serious misgivings not about her ability to pull it off but about the chance that she might inadvertently give the police some thread of a pattern that they could piece back to her.

Maybe the answer was to send her to the bottom of the outer harbor someday when she was out in that boat. It didn't particularly bother her whether it looked accidental or foul. What was important, she intuitively felt, was to avoid a pattern.

The woman pondered some more and knew the time to act was upon her. It wouldn't do to remain a female Hamlet or Prufrock. The moment had been pushed to a crisis and she would act.

She wished she could tell someone that none of this was for herself. It was all for those poor souls persecuted in 1692, particularly one of them.

The woman with the classic profile bowed her head and thought back to 1692 to what it was like.

With his cudgel, High Sheriff George Corwin prodded the backside of the last of the unfortunates as, with staggering step, she climbed into the cart. He then chained her to the other seven. Stepping back, he regarded his wagon of con-demned, seven witches and a wizard, a sneer playing on his lips. This was the biggest load yet, bigger even than the bundles of five scum each in July and August.

His eyes roved the eight. In his mind, they were consorts to the devil, tor-menters of children, and when he pushed them from the ladder, one at a time, and watched them do the air dance his heart would feel no pity. Instead, he would know only triumph and joy at ridding Salem of these scourges.

The woman with the classic profile hated George Corwin for what he had done just as she hated the girls who had done the calling out or accusing and the pious people of Salem Town and Salem Village and those other nearby commu-nities who had been so blind and hateful and stupid and she hated the magistrates who had condemned those poor souls to the noose and she hated the people in Salem today who would capitalize on and profit from those sorry old bones but she would stop all of that and she would stop those who would meddle or got in her way.

Her body was rigid and her lips quivered. She wanted to scream but no sound could escape. She put her hands to her neck and tried to stop the great pain in her throat.

She bowed her head until the pain eased and she was back in the cart staring with proud and defiant eyes at George Corwin.

"You, there," George Corwin said, staring at her. "I advise you best not be regarding me with baleful eyes. Pray to your master or do whatever you do for him to help you. Better than that, renounce him and pray to God for mercy on your soul for soon enough you be face to face with Him before you be banished from His pure eyes forever."

Beside her, a stout woman slumped over, sniveled, and then great sobs wracked her. She knew her to be Martha Cory. Her husband, a wife beater, had been crushed to death on Monday, just three days past, because he wouldn't plead. The gaoler had told them, his eyes brimming with happy expectation at the reaction his pronouncement would bring. He also told them that this pig, this Sheriff Corwin, had, with his cane, shoved poor Giles Cory's tongue back into his throat as the man gasped his death throes.

Beside Martha Cory stood frail Mary Esty, her lips moving in prayer. The woman knew her to be a good person, pious and God-fearing. Her sister, Rebecca Nurse, had been hanged in July and Sarah Cloyce, her other sister, wait-ed in the gaol for her own day with the hangman. Three good women, the Towne sisters, no more witches than . . . well, not than herself. The woman had practiced magic but what was the harm? None to herself and no great harm to anyone else either. Just enough so that she could be free from bother of those who would do her harm.

She remembered that fool Mary Simms who had accused her of thievery and who had learned the price of such nonsense. She smiled as she thought of Goodwife Simms' belly pains, coming after she told her Simms would not urinate nor cacare again until she let the woman alone.

She looked back at the pig Corwin. She would like to work magic on him so that he would never piss or cacare again and his hog belly would swell and burst. She worked the juices in her mouth and, looking him direct in the eye, spat forcefully but the glob passed by his head and rolled in the dirt.

He smiled at her and prodded the oxen. The cart rumbled, raising little clouds of dust. It squeaked and rattled as it bumped past the field where Giles Cory had died, the apple trees swaying against the leaden sky, their leaves already beginning to turn; past the Court House where they had been doomed; past the stony faces of the good people of Salem whose countenances betrayed their pious pleasure at watching someone else's last moments. But something else was written on their faces and lurked in their eyes and the woman knew what it was. It was fear, fear that they, too, might be called out for no one was safe from the hysteria and the screams and the pointing fingers of the girls who had accused scores and, before today, had sent eleven to the gallows.

Now they were bumping and swaying past Magistrate Corwin's home, uncle to the sheriff who was leading the cart. She looked at the home—it was a fine one—and for a sign of the magistrate. Maybe he would be at the hill to see the justice he and the others had meted out.

She could smell the sea. She had lived by it. The air had turned chill and she shivered. Someone was moaning in the cart and Mary Esty was still praying. Mary looked at her and smiled.

A dog was beside the cart barking at the wheels. The woman looked at the dog, a large black thing with a white splotch on its chest and it ran off behind the cart and sniffed a lump of manure dropped by one of the oxen.

After a half mile, the cart turned right down a gentle slope. At the foot and to the left the woman saw the hill. During the whole slow descent to the small bridge spanning the river, her eyes never left the hill.

The cart rumbled over the wooden staves of the bridge and turned left to make the climb to the hill and the tree that awaited them. Corwin's voice cracked at the oxen and his cudgel prodded them. The beasts strained at their yokes and the cart began its climb.

It lurched and then stopped, leaning to the left. The eight wretches in the cart slumped against their chains. Someone moaned, another sobbed, and Mary Esty still prayed.

Corwin berated the oxen with words and his stick and the brutes, wide-eyed and bellowing, dug their hooves deep into the dirt and stones but the cart clung to its place.

Men broke from the crowd that had been following the cart, a crowd filled with anticipation, a crowd released from the usual daily hard toil of survival. The men put sturdy shoulders to the cart while the women and children hung back, fearful of their men's proximity to so many intimates of Satan, still dangerous even though chained, even though in their final moments.

The men pushed, the oxen pulled, and George Corwin prodded and urged. A woman in the crowd screamed, "See, it is Satan holds back the cart. He helps his own."

At her words, several of the men stood away from the cart, but just as they did it broke free and began to lumber back up the hill again.

At the crest, the cart stopped. With the cessation of the grinding and screeching of the cart's wheels, the world seemed suddenly silent to the woman.

No, there were sounds. The oxen breathed deeply from their labors. A bird trilled its territorial song. And, still constant, Mary Esty prayed.

The tree jutted against the sky maybe 50 feet away. From a long, sturdy, nearly horizontal limb, eight nooses gently swayed. A ladder leaned against the tree.

The woman looked about her. Standing near the tree, among others, she recognized the Reverend Nicholas Noyes, present at the trials, an inquisitor, always demanding that the accused confess and repent. She had heard that Sarah Good, executed in July, had cursed Noyes, saying that if she were executed, he would drink blood. He hadn't yet, but maybe that day would come.

Behind the cart stood the citizens of Salem, silent now as if at prayer, as indeed in a way they were for Mary Esty still prayed. The woman recognized some of the accusers. There stood the Putnams, mother and daughter, one a woman, the other a child; Sarah Churchill, no longer a child; and Abigail Williams, with her uncle, the Reverend Samuel Parris of Salem Village.

Behind the throng, the woman looked at the hill sloping down to the river, winding to the sea. She sensed rain in the air and indeed even the hint of winter for this was September 22 and summer was over. But maybe her chill was for some other reason.

She looked at Corwin who was, in turn, looking at his cart-load seeming to make a choice. Their eyes locked and he smiled at her. Then he pointed at her and approached the cart, his key to the chains glinting as it captured a slash of sun-

light breaking through the clouds.

The woman sat upright, holding her throat, vainly trying to kill the streaks of pain that choked her and threatened to explode through her skull. A scream escaped, and quelled to a moan as she sat and rocked back and forth in her room.

Chapter Sixteen

Paul Clarke picked up Jan Reuter at the British Airways gate at Logan Airport at 6:45 on an evening when the weather had turned sultry again. Driving into Boston was a major motor trek for Paul Clarke, an adventure filled with both exciting and scary moments.

The mere sight and sound of jets taking off and landing was grimly fascinating, exhilarating yet terrifying. Paul Clarke had never flown and was very certain he never would.

Just negotiating his way to the terminal through the kamikaze traffic had been harrowing. Almost as unnerving was braving the admonitions of the state trooper, looking like an SS man, who told him to keep moving when he tried to double park. It took four loops before Jan Reuter appeared on the sidewalk with his suitcase. Paul Clarke was by that time sweating and wilted. The air conditioning on the old Chevy Celebrity had long ago retired.

The state trooper's stern glance as Paul Clarke pulled to the curb softened when he spotted Jan Reuter's collar and he actually graced them with a smile as they pulled away.

"Fascist," Paul Clarke muttered softly as he clenched the wheel in a death grip and made his way into the maelstrom of lunatic traffic. When they made it to the relative serenity of the road to the North Shore, he smiled at Jan Reuter and asked, "Did you have a comfortable flight?"

"Yes, thank you. I read and listened to music. God knows I couldn't watch the movie." He waved his hand. "It was intolerable."

Paul Clarke smiled as if he had first hand familiarity with the various conditions of airline travel.

"And everything went well?"

"Everything went very well."

They drove for several moments as Paul Clarke waited for elaboration. Jan Reuter was being uncharacteristically reticent. Perhaps he was tired from the flight but flying east to west shouldn't produce jet lag.

A horn blared, frightening Paul Clarke from the passing lane where he had been wallowing back to the center lane. A small red car rocketed past, leading a pent-up procession that the Celebrity had been blocking. Paul Clarke detected several withering stares and at least two obscene gestures from the drivers he had been impeding.

"So, how was his Eminence?" he asked when he had recovered.

"His Eminence was fine. Just fine. Very supportive. But I think the one on one was extremely important for him to understand fully the ramifications of the situation."

Paul Clarke nodded. "Uh, the . . ." He paused a moment. "The skull arrived."

"Good. That's settled. It very likely will be unnecessary to have it but it was a loose end. I mean having the skull-less skeleton."

"So we say, what, that we were digging around a little where the skeletons were and came up with it?"

"Yes. That should take some of the steam out of the Waters girl's theory that one of the skeleton's was the headless George Burroughs and, by extension, that the other skeletons belonged to the witchcraft hysteria victims."

"Speaking of which, they're ready for delivery at any time now."

"I'll get on that first thing tomorrow. Obviously, first we want the burial area prepared and the caskets built."

"Yes. I've spoken to Lincoln Southwick about the caskets. He's ready to start on them."

"Things are working out, I think. Finally. Shortly, we'll be able to put this matter to rest. And, I might add, get some rest ourselves."

Paul Clarke stopped for a red light near the Wonderland dog track. "What about Helen Waters and her archaeologist friend? I'm afraid that they're not likely to let the matter rest."

Jan Reuter pursed his lips in distaste as he looked at the dog track and the throngs of people eagerly flocking to it.

"First things first," he said. "Let's get the skeletons properly buried. Then we'll worry about Helen Waters and her 'friend.'"

Traffic moved as the light turned green.

"I'll tell you this. I didn't go all the way to England to meet with the Archbishop of Canterbury and I didn't go through all the rest of it—the skull, the caskets, the digging up the church basement—to let that meddlesome woman and her friend, Mr. Sennot, poke around where they don't belong and stir things up that shouldn't be."

He looked at Paul Clarke. "Don't you worry. We'll do what it takes."

In the small room that qualified as his office in the basement of the State House across from Boston Common, Joe Sennot studied the pewter cup with only a fraction of the interest that he would normally have felt. It was plain, devoid of any identifying or defining marks but Joe would have bet confidently that it dated back to the mid-18th century, probably just about the time that Boston was beginning to seethe with resentment over the taxation policies of King George the Third.

The cup had been unearthed during a major construction project near what had been the waterfront before extensive landfilling in the mid-1800s. Joe was fascinated with the Revolutionary War era and any artifacts associated with it. The reason he was unable to feel his usual ardor for an interesting artifact that just maybe was used by a participant in the Boston Massacre or the Boston Tea Party was that he was quite filled with another and most delightful ardor that was making it very difficult to feel much for anything else.

The object of his ardor was Helen Waters. Joe knew that he was hopelessly smitten, consumed by thoughts of her, engulfed by love.

By no means was Helen his first love, even discounting boyhood puppy loves and adolescent bouts of overwhelming passion.

There had been several women in his adult years, with one or two who would have qualified as "loves" and not just lovers. But he couldn't recall any previous feelings like those he held for Helen. Certainly this love now was passion but it was also pure and selfless, the stuff of poetry if he were capable of penning a poem.

But he knew he was no poet so he contented himself with alternating between just drifting mindlessly in his love for her or of thinking of her in concrete but prosaic terms. That—thinking of her very analytically— was what he was doing now as he held the pewter cup.

First, she was very beautiful. Flowing hair that practically glowed like buffed copper. Green eyes that he thought were in many ways like the ocean: deep but glinting as they reflected her many moods. High cheekbones, lightly freckled white skin, an aristocratic nose, a toothpaste ad smile.

And her figure. He could lose himself in thoughts of her physicality and he often did.

But after all thoughts, all imaginings, of corporeal Helen, Joe always came to the more enduring things—the personality, character, and mind of Helen Waters. This woman wasn't just a beautiful face and a double-take body.

He smiled at the pewter cup as he thought of moments with her during the past few weeks since he had met her: watching her roll a hogshead up the ramp from her boat; verbally and physically besting that fool Lucien Thibodeau; keeping watch over the skinheads in the Wetspot; making love to her in the dust of the church basement. He had heard that Charlie Goodwin had dubbed her "Helen Highwaters" and she lived up to the name in everyway.

His smile broadened. There was nothing ho hum about Helen Waters. His life since the short time he knew her was something he didn't want to ever change. He didn't want to go back to the pre-Helen Waters life as okay as that had been.

He thought about the implication of that sentiment. Did it mean marriage? He had always fancied bachelorhood, always pictured himself as a carefree *bon vivant*. But he'd rather spend his life with Helen Waters. Marriage, the house in the country, white picket fence, golden retriever, Volvo wagon. It now all seemed very appealing. Would it seem so to Helen?

He twirled the pewter cup and tried to concentrate on it but Helen wouldn't go away.

The whole thing had been so fast, almost like, well, like magic. That very first day he met her at the church and she invited him back to her home for lobsters he had been smitten.

He put the pewter cup down and rocked back in his swivel chair. He looked at his watch. Almost 2:30. Another hour and a half and he'd be off. Go home and shower and then drive to Stone Harbor. If traffic wasn't any worse than usual, he'd be with Helen for an evening of limitless possibilities by 6:30 at the latest.

She was well worth the drive but how much better it would be if they were living together.

As Lieutenant Michael Doyle studied the medical examiner's reports his brow furrowed in both concentration and puzzlement. Jesus, why couldn't things be simple? The only thing clear-cut about the reports was that they almost definitely linked the deaths of Reverend Fred Whittaker and Angelo Nolan.

Both men had been poisoned but by what wasn't clear except that whatever it was seemed to be the same in both cases.

He thought of Helen Waters being in the presence of Angelo Nolan just prior to his death. For the life of him he couldn't fathom Helen as a killer but he had been a cop long enough to know that absolutely nothing could be discounted. Surprises were a way of life for the cop who thought he could tell for sure who had done what or who was likely or unlikely to do this, that, or the other. Still, what would be her connection to the Reverend Whittaker?

He picked up his phone, punched some numbers and waited through four rings before he got an answer from a live voice. He had expected an answering machine.

"Doctor Robert O'Meara, please. It's Lieutenant Doyle, Salem Police."

He was put on hold and waited through several seconds of electronic-process noise. His thoughts drifted back to Helen Waters and quickly leaped from her as possible suspect to her as his former partner. His former gorgeous partner. He smiled at the recollection and was starting to savor some moments that at the time seemed as though they might lead to something quite nice when a crusty voice intruded.

"Yeah, Mike. Doc O'Meara."

"Ah, doctor, doctor. You're not making my life any simpler."

"What're you talking about?"

"I'm right now looking at your reports on the p.m.'s of Reverend Whittaker and Angelo Nolan. Doc, these things are supposed to clarify the situation for dumb cops like me but I gotta tell you I'm flat out confused. And you wanna know why? Because it looks like to me that you are confused."

He heard Doctor O'Meara chuckle dryly. "Give yourself credit, Mike. You're very observant. I am confused. As you can see on the reports, I've sent blood and tissue samples to the state lab. Call it what you want—covering your ass, passing the buck—but I'm afraid you're right, it's beyond me what did those two guys in."

Mike Doyle leaned forward in his swivel chair and arranged the reports flat on his desk in front of him. "Let's see if I've got this straight," he said. "You know, I'm trying to cut through the medicalese. The victims' symptoms and probable rapidity of death indicate the toxin was succinylcholine. The tests which indicate the toxin itself, however, indicate something resembling succinylcholine but not actually succinylcholine." Each time Mike Doyle said 'succinylcholine' he tripped through it syllable by syllable.

"Doc, what the hell is succinylcholine?"

"Curare."

"Why the hell couldn't you just say that?"

"How else are we going to impress you with how bright we are? Come on, Mike you cops have your jargon, we have ours."

"Curare, huh?" Mike Doyle said.

"Well, as I said in the report, close but not actually curare. I mean chemically close."

"Geez, with curare, you gotta use a goddamn blowgun, don't you?"

"You're right. That's part of what I mean when I say they're close but not exactly the same. Curare has to be injected. It has to get into the bloodstream somehow. It's harmless when swallowed. This stuff was ingested. Swallowed."

"Unless, of course, I imagine, the victim has a cut in his mouth or throat. Then curare would do the trick," Mike Doyle said.

"We checked for that. Or a bleeding ulcer but we checked for that too. Negative. Don't forget, the killer would have to know that the victim has that kind of condition. But we stray. It wasn't curare."

"Okay. You say in your report that reaction time and symptoms resemble poisoning by succinylcholine."

"Well, probable reaction time," Doctor O'Meara said. "We don't know exactly but there are indications that this stuff acts very, very fast. Like curare. With curare the onset of symptoms is almost instantaneous. To the point that there is no antidote. Now, something ingested or swallowed will necessarily be slower and that time will vary depending on stomach contents."

Mike Doyle looked down at the reports. "So, Reverend Whittaker probably died more quickly than Angelo Nolan."

"Right. Reverend Whittaker's stomach was nearly empty except for some wine. Angelo Nolan's was relatively full. By the way, he was a junk food devotee. Had a lot of beer nuts at the Wet Spot and had eaten before that. Submarine sandwich, chips."

"Hot peppers on the sub?"

"Huh?"

"Forget it. Christ, how do you guys do that stuff?"

"Be glad we do."

"Oh, I am. I am. But I just don't know where to go from here, know what I'm saying? I mean it's hard to start the trace on a poison if you don't even know what the hell it is. With rat poison or something like that, you at least have a place to start looking. Like your local hardware store."

"Well, Mike, this probably won't make your day but I'd start looking anyway because for some reason I've got the feeling that this won't be the last you'll see use of this stuff."

The woman with the classic profile finished meditating and went to her living room where she checked the flowering plant luxuriating in the full sun of a southern exposure. It was a pretty plant with dark-green, shiny leaves and deep-purple flowers. It stood about fifteen inches high with an almost two-foot spread. It favored the air with a faint but pleasant perfume.

The few guests she had in the time she had the plant, almost a year, had commented on how unusual it was and how pretty it was and wondered where she had gotten it.

From South America, she would reply and indeed she had gotten it from

Brazil near the border of Colombia. When she had brought it back on the plane, it was small enough to fit in her carry-on and show only as an inconclusive, innocuous blob amongst equally innocuous toilet articles on the airport X-ray. Not that she was trying to smuggle it back home or had in mind any nefarious purpose for it, but she was unsure whether there were any regulations forbidding exotic plants as there were with animals.

How she had obtained it was remarkable, she admitted to herself, almost as remarkable as what the plant could do if you knew how to prepare and use it which, as far as she knew, except for one and he was deep in the Amazonian jungles, no other white person on the planet did. That, too, was quite remarkable.

She had been on a twenty-one day river tour advertised as an Indiana Jones type adventure to remote parts of Brazil, a place she had always wanted to see, lately with increasing urgency before all the rain forest was burned down.

The tour group was relatively small and one of the guides was fluent with the various Indian dialects of the area.

Toward the end of the second week, they steamed up a tributary along which their guides informed them lived a tribe with virtually no contact with the outside world and whose future existence was at stake.

The guides assured them the tribe was peaceful and that this was a marvelous opportunity, perhaps one of the last anyone would have, to meet a people who were living the way their ancestors had for thousands of years and the way the ancestors of all humanity had once lived.

She was unsure how credible the tour guides' hype was. When they finally encountered the tribe, naked one and all, children peeking shyly at them from behind jungle brush, fearsome men with painted faces and filed teeth, placid women nursing babes and doing hard womanly work, she became convinced of the authenticity of their primitiveness and, after overcoming her fear, envisioned herself writing a Margaret Mead type book about her experience when she returned home.

They mingled with the tribe for three days, taking pictures, communicating through the fluent guide who, it turned out, had some difficulty with the language, and generally wallowed in the experience. They were titillated by their proximity to so much actual nakedness and perceived danger. They spent restless nights on the riverboat.

On the third day, emboldened and finally convinced that her head wouldn't be shrunk nor her body boiled, she drifted to the edge of the village near the rain forest where she was attracted to the beauty of a small bush with shiny dark leaves and gorgeous purple flowers. She had no idea what it was but thought it would make a marvelous souvenir and extremely attractive houseplant.

She caught the attention of a native woman in front of a nearby hut who was busy pounding a plant stalk into some kind of concoction and pointed to the flowering shrub. The native woman smiled and shook her head. She smiled in return and walked to find the fluent tour guide.

She took him to the plant and asked him if he knew what it was. He told her he didn't, that he had never seen one like it before, which surprised him as he was generally familiar with the flora and fauna of the region. She told him she'd like a rooted cutting but didn't want just to dig it up without asking a tribe member's permission.

As the guide and the native woman discussed this, the woman at first smiled then looked serious and talked animatedly with the guide. Finally, he dug a small rooted section for her, maybe three inches tall.

"I don't know how much stock to put into this," he said, "but she claims the plant can be very dangerous. Very, very poisonous."

The woman with the classic profile recoiled from it a bit. "Oh, then, I certainly don't want it."

"She says it is harmless unless you boil the leaves. The extract that comes from boiling them is deadly. Not to the touch. You'd have to drink it."

"Well, I'm certainly not planning on doing that."

"As I say, I don't know how true what she says is. I've never seen this kind of plant before and I haven't heard of any poison like that."

"Well, it's awfully pretty and I've got the perfect window for it back home if I can manage to keep it alive."

The plant proved quite hardy and she had little difficulty keeping it alive in the small drinking pot the native woman gave her, who found it very amusing to see a pot used for such a purpose.

So the plant made it all the way back home where it flourished in her window with regular watering and liquid fertilizer.

Now, as she thought about it, it was really quite fortunate that she never told anyone about its supposed strange but lethal qualities and actually almost forgot about that aspect of the plant until the unforeseen discovery of the skeletons in the church basement and Fred Whittaker's plans for them compelled her to take action she once would never have believed herself capable of.

Skeptically, she had boiled three or four leaves until they yielded a slightly fragrant amber liquid which she put in a small dish in her yard and waited for yellow jackets to take a sip of it as they were wont to do with just about anything else you tried to eat or drink outside in the summer.

Sure enough, before long they came, buzzed around a bit, and settled in for a treat. The woman was really quite startled by what she saw. Almost immediately upon alighting into the liquid and presumably taking a little drink, the wasps quivered violently for about two seconds and then floated quietly on the liquid.

Her next experiment bothered her but it was necessary. She took her liquid in a Tupperware and some pieces of bread to a small public park and found a bench in a corner away from any prying eyes except for those of the pigeons and squirrels. Wearing latex gloves, she rolled pieces of bread into marble-sized balls and dipped them into the liquid. She flung them onto the grass in front of her and waited. Her wait was brief, for soon the pigeons landed and greedily attacked the pieces of bread, leaving nothing for the squirrel who scampered up shortly after. She had always been fond of squirrels but she steeled herself into tossing him a piece of the treated bread.

For about two minutes, the pigeons and squirrel continued to watch her hopefully for further treats while she almost prayed that what she had was simply an insecticide.

Suddenly, almost in unison, the pigeons stumbled, quivered a bit and then lay still. About a half minute later the squirrel did likewise.

The woman looked about and saw that no one was in sight to witness the carnage. She got up and walked back home.

My, my, my, she had thought. This is really quite remarkable. A classic case of serendipity, except, of course, for the wasps, pigeons, and the poor squirrel. But such things happened. Just look at Alexander Fleming's discovery of penicillin, she thought.

The poisoning of the creatures in the park had received a page five column in the local papers but no autopsies were performed on the hapless pigeons and squirrel and the incident was soon forgotten.

Now the woman reached through the sunshine spilling into the window and snipped five leaves from her plant. God, it was pretty. She took them to her kitchen, put them into a pot of water on her stove and turned on the gas burner.

Then she sat down to the novel she had nearly finished to wait for the water to boil.

Chapter Seventeen

They walked hand in hand along one of Stone Harbor's twisting streets illuminated by street lights made to look like gas lamps past homes between two and three hundred years old. On the other side of the street, waves softly splashed against large stones as they had for millennia. The air was still and chilly, hinting of fall. The smell of a wood fire keeping someone snug as they looked out at the harbor was both a complement and counterpoint to the chill.

They were heading for a small restaurant built up on pilings over the stones and the waves that had very passable fish or clam chowder, although not as good as Mabel Waters'. This is a night made for chowder and beer and sitting by the window looking at the moon glinting off the ocean, Joe had said when he came to pick up Helen. Because it was a weeknight, the odds of getting a window table were pretty good.

Joe breathed in the chilly air smelling of salt and wood smoke and said, "God, I could live here."

Helen squeezed his hand. "It has its moments. But you're a big-city boy. You'd probably grow tired of it."

"Yeah, clean air, clean ocean water, no grid lock. Pretty dull, I guess."

They walked a few moments in silence.

"But I'm confident I could get used to it, especially with you around."

"Oh, if nothing else I'm always around if I'm not out there hauling traps."

"I mean it," Joe said. "I was toying with the idea of finding a place here to live. Actually, I've, uh, kind of fallen in love with Stone Harbor."

"Have you now?"

"Well, you know, I mean if I found the right place."

"Lodgings don't come cheap in Stone Harbor. We're a desirable community, you know."

"It can't be too bad if two share the rent."

"Oh? Who's your friend?"

Joe stopped walking and turned to her. "Helen, cut it will you. You know what I'm talking about."

"You mean us." Helen smiled but shook her head slowly. "Joe, I've got a grandmother that right now I just can't . .." Her voice trailed.

"That's it? Because of your grandmother you don't want to—?

"Live with you? You know I really care for you but this is kind of quick, Joe."

"Helen, we're not kids. I mean we've gotten to know each other really well and I certainly know how I feel."

"You mean gotten 'to know' each other in the Biblical sense?"

"Jesus, I don't mean just that."

They resumed walking and said nothing until they reached the restaurant. They got their window seat and looked out at the harbor, the flame of the candle on their table flickering its reflection in the glass.

"Helen, I wasn't just thinking of living together. I mean at first, yes, but eventually . . . " He shook his head slightly and put his hand on top hers.

"Eventually what?"

"I know how I feel, Helen, and I'm assuming, uh, I'm hoping you feel the same way."

She smiled and put her free hand on top of his. "Oh, gosh, Joe, everything's right, isn't it? Candlelight, moonlight, ocean view, but you're moving too fast for me."

A waiter smiled down at them and they ordered beer and chowder.

"Well," Joe said when the waiter had gone, "I'll move as fast or slow as you like but I just want to be with you, Helen."

"Things are fine right now with us, Joe. Give me some time. Let's see what works out." She thought of Mike Doyle and what he had said about her perhaps needing a lawyer. "Yeah, just give me a little time, Joe. That's one thing we've both got plenty of."

Lincoln Southwick looked at Jan Reuter and Paul Clarke. They both looked so damn solemn that he wanted to laugh. He hadn't seen them since the night of the attempt to burn down the church and only the recollection of his embarrassing position that night kept him from chuckling out loud.

"So, you think you can do it?" Jan Reuter said.

"No problem." Linc looked down at the plans for constructing a pine casket in front of him. "It looks pretty simple."

"How long will it take you?"

Linc scratched his head. "Hmmm. Once I get the stock, I dunno, probably less than a week. I figure I can do four a day once I get rolling."

"Good," Jan Reuter said. "You order the stock, will you, have it shipped here. You can use the basement to work in. Just bring your tools over. Can you do all that today?"

Linc looked at his watch. Just a little after nine on a beautiful morning but a little earlier than he was used to rising. "Sure. You know, it's kind of funny, but I'm the guy who dug 'em up, I mean in a way, and now I'm the guy who's gonna rebury them or at least build their caskets."

"I suppose there is a certain irony," Jan Reuter said. He stirred in his seat impatiently. "I'd really like you to get started today. I mean on the actual building."

Linc nodded. "Sure, I can do that. Get at least one done after lunch." He shuffled a work-booted foot across the Oriental rug. "I just don't get what the big rush is. I mean after all these years that the skeletons were unburied."

"Those people were Christians," Jan Reuter said. "Don't you think it's high time they got some rest?"

Linc thought of the restaurant he was planning. He'd love to have one of the skeletons to put in a glass case near the front door. What a draw that would be. He wondered if he could maybe sneak at least a couple of bones when the skeletons came back.

He managed a solemn expression. "Oh, sure. That's the least we can do, make sure they get a good rest."

When Lincoln Southwick had left, Paul Clarke shook his head doubtfully and clenched his bony hands nervously. "Do you think he's to be trusted? I really have my doubts."

"Someone's got to do the work. I feel with him, at least, I have some control," Jan Reuter said.

"You mean because . . . "

Jan Reuter nodded. "Yes, because of his little indiscretion a few years back."

"For which he came to you for counseling."

"Poor man fell prey to the callings of the flesh." Jan Reuter smiled pontifically. "As did our departed friend and colleague, Fred Whittaker, I'm afraid."

"In Southwick's case it was a special problem," Paul Clarke said. "I mean the woman wasn't legally a woman."

"It wasn't even close. Fourteen is a bit tender. Winsome thing, though, wasn't she?"

"What bothers me," Paul Clarke said, "is that what got Southwick in trouble there is still a problem. The man drinks and when he does there's apparently no controlling what he says or does."

"Look, he owes me. Forget about humiliation, he was facing serious jail time. Fortunately for him, I was able to intercede and smooth things over. He knows he's got to be discreet. But, if it makes you feel better, I'll speak to him again and spell it out that he's got to keep his mouth shut."

"This secrecy," Paul Clarke said, "it really all goes back to Philip English, doesn't it"

Jan Reuter leaned back in his leather chair and stretched his legs on the matching leather ottoman. "Yes it does. And you know how I feel about that. We absolutely must honor it. The man built this very church. He financed it."

"He had no use for the Puritans, that's certain."

"Would you have? Given what he went through because of them?" Jan Reuter shook his head sadly. "He bounced back, though, from financial ruin and the loss of his wife. He was a victim of the Puritans and so he really related to those other victims who paid for Puritanical bigotry, jealousy, and stupidity with their lives. The Puritan law was that witches could not be buried in consecrated land. They were just thrown in a pit at the foot of Gallows Hill, and their bodies lightly covered with soil. Philip English knew they were innocent souls and was determined to give them proper burial—even if he was breaking the law. He wanted their burial here kept secret—we have that in writing—and so it shall remain. Or as close to that as is now possible given all that has occurred since our Lincoln Southwick stumbled across the skeletons."

"Well, we just didn't know they were in that part of the basement. The assumption was that they were buried under the altar area. That is, if they weren't buried outside."

They sat in silence a few moments. "Something's bothering you?" Paul Clarke finally said.

"I was just thinking of George Burroughs and how all that happened to him especially troubled English. I'm glad we were able to get the skull," Jan Reuter said. He thought of the skull delivered here to Paul Clarke while he was in England, now secure in a special closet in the basement. "All those poor people were victims but that man was positively defiled by Cotton Mather and I think Philip English felt a particular empathy for him."

"No question about it."

"Think of it," Jan Reuter said, shaking his head. "Here was a man who had been minister of Salem Village before Samuel Parris. He moved to Maine yet even that distance wasn't enough to protect him from the long arm of the witch hysteria of 1692."

Paul Clarke nodded gravely. This was a story both men knew well but its repetition didn't diminish it for them in any way.

"And what a man he was," Reuter continued. "Quick witted, a virtual Samson in strength, humorous. On the gallows he flawlessly recites the Lord's Prayer, the supposed acid test of innocence, yet that archetype puritan Cotton Mather would-not be denied. 'The devil is never more treacherous than when he assumes the guise of innocence,' Mather had said, or words to that effect. And so poor Burroughs was hanged anyway."

"And Mather, thinking Burroughs was the devil reincarnate, has Burroughs's head removed to study it for signs of the devil," Paul Clarke said. "How Philip English must have hated Mather."

"Well, we're doing all that we can do. Fred Whittaker would have continued the exploitation of those unfortunate souls."

"So all we have to worry about now is the blabby mouth of Lincoln Southwick who, because of his past indiscretion, should be no problem," Paul Clarke said. He leaned away from a shaft of sunlight that made his pale rheumy eyes water. "And, of course, the troublesome Miss Waters and friend. That, I'm afraid, still bothers me."

"Not to worry, not to worry," Jan Reuter said. "There are means. I assure you, there are means."

Mary Rose O'Brine gathered the five books, new releases that would be a passport to Mabel Waters' house. Three mysteries and two non-fiction, one about Alaska, the other about the Great Depression.

"Are those for your aunt's friend?" Virginia Rowe, the other librarian on duty asked. She knew of Mary Rose's practice of bringing new books to Mabel Waters for an early reading.

"Yes. She's such an avid reader. I think it's great she hasn't had to go to large print yet."

"Nice of you to do it."

Mary Rose shrugged. "I'll probably go over this evening after work. It's pleasant. We'll sit around and chat a bit. Talk about what she's just read. Have some tea or a little wine. And it'll give me a chance to talk with my old friend Helen Waters."

"That's her granddaughter?"

"Yes," Mary Rose said smiling. "Oh, I've got to tell you. I probably shouldn't because I know Helen would be embarrassed but it's such a cute story. Mabel, you know, wants to get Helen married. So you know what she's been doing? She's been buying love potion at Loretta Lowell's shop and slipping it to Helen and her friend who, I've got to tell you, wouldn't be a bad catch."

Virginia threw back her head and laughed. "Stop it. Love potion?"

"Yes"

The two women laughed together.

"What is it, this love potion?"

"Oh, gosh, I don't know. Crushed snails or toads or something."

"Oh, God." Virginia laughed some more. Then she became serious. "But I'd be careful about anything that came out of Loretta Lowell's shop. I mean with all the rumors going around that maybe somehow some witch potion could be implicated in the deaths of that minister and that other guy."

Mary Rose shook her head derisively. "I certainly don't put any stock in any of that nonsense. I'm sure Loretta Lowell is a fine person. Maybe making a little harmless money off the gullible but I'd be very surprised if anything more potent than caffeine came out of her shop."

"Oh, I'm sure," Virginia said. "But if Helen gets married, let me know will you. I've got someone in mind that I'd like to try that potion on."

Helen brought her catch in, talked with Charlie Goodwin a while, and went home and showered. Her grandmother was out. A note on the kitchen counter said she had gone for a walk, it was such a beautiful day.

After showering, she sat at the counter eating a toasted cheese and tomato sandwich and thought of last night and what Joe had said. She had been thinking about it all morning while out on the *Working Girl*. She wished he hadn't brought up the subject of their living together with a very strong hint about marriage. It wasn't a bended knee proposal but there was no mistaking his intent and the whole thing unnerved her.

She wondered about that. Why should she find what he had said so unsettling? Joe was right, they certainly weren't kids. Living with a guy before marriage had long ago died as a taboo and in this case, if Joe had his way, it would lead to marriage.

Was she reluctant because of her grandmother? Mabel Waters was a tough old lady, very capable of living on her own, who would be the last person to be an anchor on her granddaughter.

Was she afraid of commitment? Was Joe the right guy? On paper, he had all the credentials: he was good-looking, educated, responsible, and fun to be with.

But the big question, she knew, was whether she loved him. She positively couldn't say that she didn't. Less positive but still true, she couldn't say that she did.

Maybe then living together for a while would be a good idea, a finding out process for him as well as for her.

She had told Joe that she needed some time and she had been truthful in that. She hadn't told him about Mike Doyle and the suspicions cast upon her in the Angelo Nolan murder. She doubted that Joe even knew about Nolan's death. He didn't regularly read either the Salem or Stone Harbor newspapers and the death hadn't gotten a big play in the Boston papers. No, it was obvious Joe didn't know or he would have said something.

She thought of Mike Doyle. There was no question that his telling her that she might need a lawyer and the whole unfinished business with the skeletons and the murders was part of her reluctance to commit to anything with Joe beyond what they now had.

But Mike Doyle. She remembered how she had felt when she saw him the first day she talked with him at the police station about the death of Reverend Whittaker. She remembered the night he had given her Nolan's name and the motel he was staying at on Route 1. Although she was sure she hadn't shown it, she had struggled with her feelings when Mike put his hand on hers and made an overture.

Wouldn't a true love for Joe cancel the remaining feelings she had for Mike Doyle?

"Dammit," she said aloud. She finished her sandwich and diet Coke, cleaned up the counter, left a note for her grandmother, and drove to Salem.

She looked Mike Doyle straight in the eye. They sat in his office at the Salem Police station. This time she didn't feel the warm flush. There was ice between them.

"To what do I owe this honor?" Mike Doyle said, trying for levity.

"Cut the crap, Mike. Last time I talked with you, you said next time we talked I might need a lawyer."

Mike Doyle smiled. "Did you bring one?"

"Mike, I'm not here to fool around and I know this isn't exactly routine, I mean your talking off the cuff and all with someone you regard as a suspect but we go back."

"It sure as hell isn't routine, Helen."

"But it's my life, Mike, and right now I feel everything's on hold. Every day I wait for the hammer to drop."

"What do you want from me?"

"Just tell me where things are going?"

"I can't do that. Talk sense, Helen. I've talked to you too much as it is."

Helen breathed a deep exasperated breath, held it a moment and slowly let it out."Look me in the eye, Mike, and tell me you seriously regard me as a suspect in the death of Angelo Nolan. Just do that."

Mike Doyle picked up a paper clip from his desk, bent it open, and twirled it between his thumb and forefinger. He sucked on the inside of his cheek.

"Come on, Mike. It's me. You think I'm a goddamn murderer?"

"I'll tell you this much, Helen. We now know whoever killed Angelo Nolan very, very likely killed Whittaker too."

"You believed that all along."

"Yeah, but now the lab reports pretty well confirm it."

"Come on, Mike, there's nothing there that points to me. There can't be."

Mike Doyle sucked his cheek some more and twirled the paper clip back and forth. "You been to South America lately, Helen?"

"Huh?"

"Whatever killed Whittaker and Nolan might have come from there. I say that because it's very similar to curare. Ever hear of that?"

"Curare? Sure. The natives put it on darts that they fire from blowguns. Deadly as hell, I guess. I guess you've got me, Mike. Come on over to my place, bring a warrant. I've got jars of curare all over the place."

"I said it's similar to curare but it's not curare."

Mike Doyle put the paper clip down. "I ought to have my head examined, telling you this stuff. Get the hell out of here."

"No. You don't need your head examined. The thing is you know that I had nothing to do with those murders. You're just being . . . "

"Being what?"

"Being a stubborn pain in the ass."

Mike Doyle picked the paper clip up and threw it at her. "Get out of here."

Helen bent the paper clip back to its original shape and put it on the desk. She leaned across and kissed Mike Doyle on the cheek. "Thanks, Mike."

"For what?" he said sharply.

"For showing a little faith in me. For treating me like your former partner, someone you trust, rather than a suspect."

"Helen, I assure you—"

She was still leaning across the desk and she kissed him again on the cheek but a little closer to the mouth. "You have assured me."

She pulled away. "You're sweet, Mike."

She left the station feeling she had been only partially reassured on the things that had been bothering her.

Mike Doyle put his hand to his cheek where Helen had kissed him and smiled. He wondered how he had played his cards. All right, he guessed.

He laughed when he thought of what he had said. I ought to have my head examined, telling you this stuff. Not bad, not overplayed.

But he was glad he had gone through the little charade because he was pleased with how Helen had reacted. She was right, of course. In his heart of hearts, he didn't believe she was guilty.

On the other hand, maybe she was better at acting than he was.

He sighed and picked up the paper clip she had put back on his desk.

Back home, Helen checked the answering machine but there were no messages. Her grandmother hadn't returned from her walk so she sat in the front window and looked out to the street.

'Curare,' she thought and went to her dictionary. It didn't tell her anything revealing beyond what she already knew. She mulled 'curare' and then thought about Mike Doyle for a few moments. Best to drive Mike Doyle from her mind except as a police officer. Not best to, had to. He was a married man and there was no way she was going to get involved in any of that.

Then she thought about Joe and the fact that he hadn't called and left a message. He always did that, letting her know whether he'd be by that evening.

She found that she was a little miffed that he hadn't called and hoped that he would. She wanted to go out with him this evening. She smiled to herself. She was acting like a schoolgirl.

Maybe he was hurt by her reaction or lack of it last night. But if he loved her the way he said he did, he should not be deterred.

They hadn't made love last night after they left the restaurant but often they didn't. They couldn't do that in his car and they were reluctant to at Helen's house because they never knew for sure whether her grandmother was awake or asleep. Occasionally they visited the *Working Girl* but its fishy smell left a lot to be desired as a crib of romance. Often they joked about needing the church basement again. From a logistical point of view, if they were to continue seeing each other, living together made sense.

The phone rang. She smiled and her heart sang as she answered it but it was Mary Rose O'Brine. She wanted to know if this evening would be convenient to drop off some new books for Mabel. Helen said that it would be fine. They chatted for a few moments.

When she hung up, Helen made herself a cup of tea and continued to look out the window for her grandmother. This was a long walk Mabel was taking and Helen felt a tinge of concern. Her mind began to play with all kinds of possibilities, none of them pleasant.

The ringing phone chilled her.

It was Joe. They cooed for a few minutes and then made plans for the evening. "I think I'd like to visit the *Working Girl* tonight, smell or no smell," Joe said.

"I guess that can be arranged. Oh, I should tell you, we might be a few minutes getting away. Mary Rose O'Brine is dropping by with some library books for my grandmother. You've met her. Usually she chats for a while but she won't stay too long."

They talked for a few more minutes, neither wanting to let go, until Mabel Waters walked in the front door and smiled approvingly when she determined the caller was Joe.

Let people say what they want about Wicca, she thought, for her money Loretta Lowell was a miracle worker.

Malvina Drinan left work about an hour early, complaining of a headache, which she actually did have. But that wasn't the main reason for her early departure.

She wanted to make sure she had time to get everything ready. This was an important night. There were things that had to be said exactly right and done exactly right and she wanted to give herself time to go over all of that in her mind.

Also, she had to factor in travel time and what to do if the unexpected occurred, which it always seemed to do.

She let herself into her four-room apartment, went straight for the bathroom where she took three aspirin and a long, warm shower which she tapered off to as icy a blast as she could stand.

She put on fresh clothes and wet brushed her long, straight hair.

She checked her watch, felt a shudder of anticipation for the evening, and went into her kitchen.

Chapter Eighteen

The woman with the classic profile went to her refrigerator for the vial of extract she had boiled from the leaves of the pretty plant in her living room window. She had done some further experimenting with the extract on insects and found that it retained its potency better if refrigerated. She imagined that the tribe in Brazil, if they used the stuff, must have to use it quickly in the heat of the rain forest.

Now she had to do something she was reluctant to do but she felt it was necessary. The pretty plant in the living room had to go. Getting rid of it was like burning a bridge behind her but after tonight she'd have no further need for its special quality.

There were other reasons for her reluctance to get rid of the plant. One, she was fond of it. It reminded her of the marvelous time she had had on the trip. And it was so pretty.

Two, it probably should be introduced to the scientific community, particularly the medical community. She felt the chances were high that in much diluted form the extract would have medical applications. This concerned her. She shook her head. It was too bad.

Taking a plastic trash bag from a drawer, she went to the living room window where the plant luxuriated. She hesitated a moment and then with a sigh deposited it in the trash bag.

Goddamn the police. It was their fault she had to do this. They had been by to question her shortly after Angelo Nolan's death. It was perverse. A predator like that flourished with impunity—never a cop in sight when he did his thing—but let anything happen to him and the cops were on the scene in a blink.

There was no question he had to be disposed of. First, he might connect her to Fred Whittaker. There was always the chance he had seen her in Fred's company and gotten a really good look at her. Second, the man just plain deserved to die. His witch bashing was an abomination not that personal retribution had anything to do with her motive. She was above that.

Getting to know Angelo Nolan on a friendly basis hadn't been easy because she was a bit too plump for Angelo's taste. She was honest with herself on that point. Most men were such pigs. Physicality was all that mattered to them. Still, she did what it took to gain his 'affection', she guessed she'd have to call it, for want of a better word. It had been disgusting.

She had taken to spending some time at the Wet Spot when she learned it was a favorite spot of Angelo's and his two friends who also deserved to die in her estimation but you had to pick your shots and be cautious of overkill. When she'd go there, she changed her appearance as much as possible. But, hell, a different hairstyle and a lot of make up made a huge difference. Imagine her surprise when who should walk in the very night she planned to send Angelo Nolan the way of Fred Whittaker but Helen Waters and her boyfriend. She had had to hide in the ladies room and when they left she didn't have much time to slip Angelo his little drink. Fortunately, he and his buddies and the harlots with them were too far-gone to notice what she was doing.

When Angelo and his buddies left, she followed discreetly and, when Angelo took a nosedive into the sidewalk, she told them to tell the police that a Helen Waters said to Angelo in The Wetspot, 'How's your face feel? I'm going to give you a real taste of something?"

She was pleasantly surprised when Kyle and Tommy told her they gave the line to the police. She wished she could have seen Helen squirm on that one. Probably the bitch didn't have to squirm, being an ex-cop and all.

She squeezed the plastic vial. No matter. After tonight, Helen Waters wouldn't be squirming or doing anything at all.

Tommy Crawford and Kyle Peterson sat in Tommy's ten year old Trans Am, a faded, rusted hulk that still made nice rumbling sounds in Tommy's estimation and still moved out pretty quick and attracted a certain class of chick, a bit on the young side, but that didn't bother Tommy. The Blazer had belonged to Angie and now resided at his mom's home in Charlestown. But Tommy had never liked the Blazer or any of that kind of off-road vehicle, anyway. Too yuppyish for his money. You want to haul ass, there was nothing like a 350 under your foot hitched to a nice rear drive hooked up to a pair of 245/50ZR-16's.

They were parked by the waterfront, the Trans Am looking a tad out of place amongst the Cherokees and Volvos, figuring out just how to make their move. They wanted to settle with the babe who had done Angie in. They knew her name, they knew she lived in Stone Harbor, they knew she drove an old Chevy pick-up, and they knew she had a boat called the *Working Girl*. They also knew she was damned good looking because they had seen her that night at The Wetspot. It was a shame in a way that she was such a nice looking piece but when they were done with her she wouldn't be good looking at all.

They had looked up Waters in the phone book, found only one, an M. Waters, and had driven by the house. Bingo! The Chevy truck was in the driveway. Then they drove around, finally settling into a spot by the waterfront. They had dined on submarine sandwiches, chips, and split a six pack of beer, none of the local sailboat yuppie stuff. Good old red-blooded Bud was fine with them, thank you.

"What pisses me," Tommy was saying, "is she can't try something to your face, know what I mean? Friggin' poison. How sneaky is that?"

"Poor Angie," Kyle said. "He was cool. He didn't deserve to die like a poisoned rat. The Reverend either."

"Yeah, he was okay," Tommy said. "I mean, for a reverend, he was one funny bastard."

Neither Tommy nor Kyle had known Fred Whittaker well. Angie had met him one night while the Reverend Fred Whittaker was cruising various clubs in Boston, attired in very non-reverend clothes and trying to strike the acquaintance in a non-pastoral way of college girls.

As it turned out, he and Angie were bar leaning, each eyeing the same young things sitting at a table laughing and drinking and looking ever so fetching. Fred and Angie struck up a conversation and Fred Whittaker actually bought Angie a drink.

One drink led to another and the conversation eventually revealed that Angelo Nolan might have qualities and talents that Fred Whittaker could use in his ever-increasing hostility with the practitioners of Wicca in Salem. He invited Angie up to Salem where they finally settled a working relationship. Tommy and Kyle were Angie's associates in his strong-arm activities but they got to know the Reverend only casually, Fred Whittaker naturally being very cautious about direct contact with such types, at least in Salem.

So now Tommy and Kyle sat in Tommy's Trans Am by the quaint and picturesque waterfront waiting to bring about some kind of closure to their Salem and Stone Harbor activities.

It was time to settle accounts with the person who had, in a most sneaky way, offed their friend Angelo Nolan and the Reverend Fred Whittaker.

Malvina Drinan checked herself in the mirror, took a deep breath, opened her bag and checked the contents again. All was set. A short walk to the bus stop and she'd be in Stone Harbor within twenty minutes.

She touched the unicorn dangling at her throat. It had always brought her luck.

The table had been cleared, lamb chops rather than seafood the main course tonight for Mabel and Helen, and now Mabel poured coffee for the two of them and for Joe and Mary Rose who had arrived tactfully after the dinner hour, within ten minutes of each other.

They sat in the living room, a fire a cozy counterpoint to the chill outside. Mabel beamed as she poured. Things seemed to be progressing nicely with Joe and Helen and it was always nice to have Mary Rose for company. She was so well read.

Helen sipped her coffee, She looked at Joe and thought of the two of them later on in the chill and stink of the *Working Girl*. She shivered and wrinkled her nose.

Maybe it was time to sell the *Working Girl*. Trouble was, no one wanted to buy a fishing boat today with the uncertainty of fishing what it was.

She looked at Joe. He looked good. What the hell. Sell the *Working Girl,* cut her losses, become a teacher and Mrs. Joseph Sennot. She could do a lot worse.

Mary Rose was saying something and Helen tried to focus. Mabel had her talking about her recent vacation. Mary Rose travled just about everywhere, places civilized and uncivilized. She sat in that library and read about exotic locations and saved her money so that she could visit them. Helen felt a twinge of envy and tried to remember where Mary Rose had last visited. The girl had climbed mountains, sailed rivers, walked the Great Wall of China, even.

But she hadn't had Joe Sennot propose to her.

The phone rang and Mabel answered it in the kitchen. It was for Helen. "It's a man," Mabel said with a shrug, handing the phone to Helen.

"Is this Helen Waters who owns the *Working Girl*?" the man's voice asked.

When Helen said it was, the man hung up. Unsettled, Helen came back to the living room.

"Crank call," she said. She eyed the books on the coffee table Mary Rose had brought for her grandmother. They were in their plastic covers and the page edges were stamped Salem Public Library but they had that look of newness about them. Mabel Waters would be their first reader. Something about the books tickled Helen's memory but she couldn't place what it was. She stood and leaned forward to see the titles and as she did she looked out the living room window to the street and the driveway.

"Where's your car, Mary Rose?" she asked.

Mary Rose smiled and waved her hand. "That old thing. It's in the garage having a little work done. I took the bus."

"You should have told me. I'd have picked you up."

"Don't be silly."

"Well, at least let us give you a ride home whenever you're ready."

"I appreciate it but in a little while I'm going to take a stroll through town and check out an antique shop or two."

They all chatted for a moment about antiques until Mabel went back to the kitchen to get the pot of coffee for re-fills. Quickly, Mary Rose followed saying that her Aunt Ione wanted her to get a particular recipe from Mabel.

Joe and Helen sat, looking at the fire and one another.

"It's going to be cold tonight on the *Working Girl*," Helen said, keeping her voice low. She wondered about the call she just got. She should check out the *Working Girl* to make sure it was okay.

Joe shrugged. "If you don't—"

"What I was thinking, is that maybe we should start looking for a nice place here in Stone Harbor to share as you suggested last night."

"You mean—"

"I mean see where it takes us."

Joe beamed. "When?"

"I'll start checking out ads and go see a realtor tomorrow. That is, if I don't catch pneumonia tonight on the *Working Girl*."

Tommy Crawford's plan was simple. He and Kyle would park as close to the Waters babe's house as possible and keep an eye on the front door. When she came out, they'd follow and when the chance allowed they'd do what they came to do. If she didn't come out, they'd wait until very late, go to the door and when she answered they'd be in in a flash. He knew she was at home because he had just called and asked if she was the Helen Waters who owned the *Working Girl*.

He parked the Trans Am where he had a good shot at the Waters house. He and Kyle sat and smoked and occasionally took out and fondled the long and very sharp knives they kept sheathed in their boots.

Jan Reuter and Paul Clarke stood in the basement of their church amidst the bundles of wood and the power tools that belonged to Lincoln Southwick. A sprinkle of sawdust made the floor slippery and scented the air.

They looked at Linc's production for the day: two completed pine caskets. He had said he'd probably be able to complete four a day and that appeared to be on target considering the late start he got today.

"It won't be long now," Jan Reuter said. "We'll put those poor people to rest with a private and very appropriate ceremony. And, I hope, put the entire matter to rest."

Paul Clarke nodded.

Jan Reuter stared meditatively for a moment at the two completed caskets. Unconsciously, he slid his foot back and forth over the glaze of sawdust.

"You know what I think might be a good idea right now?" he said. "I think you and I might do well to take a little walk over to Helen Waters' home to pay her a little visit."

Malvina Drinan got off the bus near the harbor that gave Stone Harbor its name. You could smell the sea in Salem but in Stone Harbor it always seemed stronger and fresher. She was having a hard time quelling her nervousness. That was odd because she hadn't had that problem before.

Well, no matter. She was almost there. She breathed the sea water tang and walked determinedly, a woman on a mission.

Mabel brought the coffeepot back into the living room and refilled the four cups.

"Cream, anyone?" Joe said. "May I pour?"

Helen and Mabel nodded. "No thanks," Mary Rose said.

Mabel stirred in two teaspoons of sugar and handed the bowl to Helen who took just one teaspoon. Joe, also, did one.

They stirred and looked at the fire.

Helen wondered how and when to tell her grandmother that she might be moving out soon to move in with Joe. She couldn't do it now with Mary Rose present.

To make conversation, she said, "What was the recipe that your aunt wanted, Mary Rose?"

Mary Rose seemed startled by the question. "Oh, Ione just loves Mabel's cream of broccoli soup. She's been meaning to get it. I told her I was coming over tonight and that I'd ask Mabel for it."

"It's delicious, isn't it? I have to confess, though, that when I was a kid I didn't much care for it."

"It's funny that Ione never mentioned anything to me about it," Mabel said.

"Mary Rose smiled. "She's a fan of your cooking, let me tell you."

Helen smiled at her grandmother. "Everyone is a fan of your cooking."

"I certainly am," Joe said. He picked up his coffee cup.

Helen's smile faded as she looked around. Something wasn't right. She looked at Mary Rose sitting as primly as her chubbiness would allow, her round eyeglasses making her look sweet and slightly owlish as ever. She was so pretty. If only she'd do something about her weight, Helen thought.

She looked at Mary Rose's coffee cup.

What was it?

She looked at the library books on the coffee table that Mary Rose had brought for her grandmother and something clicked in her mind and then something else clicked.

Her hand shot out to Joe's arm as he brought his coffee cup to his lips, shaking his hand and spilling the coffee a little onto the rug.

"Don't drink that! Gram, don't touch yours." Helen's voice shook.

"What's the matter?" Mabel said. She laughed nervously. "Everyone likes my cooking but not my coffee?"

Helen looked at Mary Rose who was starting to get up. "Mary Rose, I don't get it. You had cream and sugar in your first cup of coffee but not the second. Why's that? Weren't you going to drink it?"

"Of course I was. I was just . . . " Her voice trailed. She seemed flustered.

"Sit down, Mary Rose. Where are you going? Tell us about your last trip. Where did you go? Somewhere in South America, wasn't it?"

Helen's voice was hard and biting.

"Helen, for God's sake," Joe said. "What's the matter with you? You're being rude."

Helen picked up one of the library books from the coffee table and thumbed through it. "Mary Rose, you know where I saw a library book like this, all new and crisp? At the Reverend Fred Whittaker's living room. He was the minister who was poisoned. You remember. Did you know him, Mary Rose? Did you bring him brand new library books to read before they got all dog eared and smudged by the general public?"

"Helen, what are you talking about?" Mabel said.

"I'm sure I don't know," Mary Rose said, standing and moving toward the door. "But I think it's time that I left."

She looked at Joe and Mabel. "I'm sorry. I don't know what's come over her."

"Wait a minute. Why don't you just sit down," Helen said, moving after her but Mary Rose had opened the door and was out with surprising speed considering her girth.

"Gram, don't drink that coffee but don't throw it away. Call the police. Joe, come help me," Helen yelled as she disappeared out the door after Mary Rose.

What the hell! Tommy Crawford and Kyle Peterson sat upright. The fat broad from The Wet Spot who told them to tell the police that Helen Waters had threatened Angie bolted out the door of the Waters home followed by Waters herself followed by the guy who had been with Waters that night at the Wet Spot.

The fat one was really hauling, considering she wasn't built like a sprinter exactly. Waters and the guy were gaining on her, though, and Waters was yelling something but Tommy and Kyle couldn't tell what it was.

"Come on," Tommy said, getting out of the Trans Am. Before they could cross the street, they had to wait a moment for a car to pass which had slowed down so that the driver could gawk at the three running figures.

Now the guy had caught up with Waters and was holding her so that she couldn't chase the fat one. They were arguing and the fatty was taking advantage to gain some more.

Tommy and Kyle crossed over but Waters and the guy were running again in pursuit.

Tommy bent over to get at his knife. "Let's get the guy first then we'll take out Waters."

"What the hell's going on?" Kyle said.

"How do I know? Shut up and let's go. Get your knife."

Five figures, feet thumping and breath condensing in rapid puffs, ran down the narrow, winding Stone Harbor street. Blades gleamed in the hands of the last two.

Ahead was an intersection and Mary Rose, with a quick glance back over her shoulder, took a sharp right and plowed into Jan Reuter and Paul Clarke, sending Paul Clarke sprawling onto the street.

Mary Rose and Jan Reuter backed dazedly away from each other as Helen and Joe came around the corner.

"Behind you, Joe, look out."

"What the—" Joe said as Tommy Crawford lunged at him. Joe caught the knife arm and the two wrestled as Helen jumped between them and Kyle Peterson.

Kyle Peterson made a sweeping arc at Helen with his knife which she ducked. She shot her hand into his face, her fingers out straight and stiff and felt them sink into the soft jelly of his eyes. He screamed, fell to the ground, and she turned and jumped onto the back of Tommy Crawford, pummeling his head with her fists and then with her open palms boxing his ears as hard as she could.

He screeched, dropped his knife and fell to the sidewalk with Joe on top of him.

Jan Reuter stood transfixed, his mouth agape. Paul Clarke sat on the street stunned. but with enough presence of mind to attempt to rearrange his dislodged strips of hair across the top of his skull.

Mary Rose leaned against a fence, breathing like a guppy out of water, totally exhausted.

"Why, Mary Rose, why?" Helen said, moving close in to the puffing Mary Rose. Mary Rose hung her head and tried to catch her breath. Helen was afraid she was going to have a heart attack. Joe came to her side with a knife in his hand.

"What about them," he said, jerking his thumb at the sprawled figures of Tommy Crawford and Kyle Peterson.

Helen smiled. "Just in time," she said. "Here comes the cavalry."

Blue light pulsed across them as a police cruiser pulled up and two cops jumped out. They moved in quickly and, when one of them looking at her with a grin said something about 'Helen Highwaters,' Helen groaned. She liked Charlie Goodwin but she'd have to speak with him for hanging that handle on her.

Malvina Drinan found him where he said he'd be in the little restaurant by the water. She'd met him just a week ago at a Wiccan meeting in Salem and they seemed to hit it off pretty well.

He was from Boston, didn't have a car, so they decided to meet again tonight by themselves at a mutually convenient place. More convenient for her than for him, actually. But he was a gentleman.

She smiled. He smiled. Unconsciously, she touched her unicorn. Her nervousness was melting. This would be a very nice evening. She was sure of it.

Chapter Nineteen

They were on the *Working Girl*, late evening, bellies full of food and bodies relaxed and glowing from several glasses of beer in Joe's case, wine in Helen's.

It was four days since Mary Rose O'Brine had been arrested.

"I talked with Mike Doyle today," Helen said. "You know, the Salem cop I told you about."

"And?"

"And he told me—off the record, of course—that the coffee tested the same as the stuff that killed Whittaker and Nolan. They don't really know what it is. Some new stuff she got in Brazil."

Helen paused. They were in the cramped hold of the *Working Girl*, with the only light from a battery-powered lantern. The air was damp and fishy smelling. The *Working Girl* rocked gently at her mooring.

"He also told me that Mary Rose has really opened up. She's held nothing back but she'll probably do some psychological evaluation time. Then, who knows? I don't know that she'll ever go to trial. I think she's a very sick person."

"Well, that's good. I mean that she's spilled all. You said the Salem cop suspected you?"

"I don't know that he ever really did. Maybe. It doesn't matter now. Mary Rose was a practitioner of Wicca and was a descendant of a woman executed in 1692. She felt that Reverend Whittaker was going to make a big, ostentatious thing about the skeletons. So she stopped him. Angelo Nolan she knew was a witch-basher and was afraid he might link her to Whittaker whom she had had an affair with. And she knew I was poking around because I thought I was a suspect. You and my grandmother were in the wrong place at the wrong time."

She looked at Joe closely. "That was close. You practically had that coffee cup to your mouth. The stuff is fast acting and deadly. We'd probably have been gone—the three of us—within ten or fifteen minutes."

"I'll say this," Joe said. "Life with you won't be dull."

He kissed her, the kiss lingering.

Then he laughed. "Sorry. But you know what was really funny? Reuter and Clarke. Did you see Clarke on the street? Mary Rose must have given him a terrific body check."

Helen laughed too. "You know what? They were coming to my house to set me straight. Lincoln Southwick is building caskets for the skeletons. They're going to rebury them with a very quiet ceremony somewhere on the church grounds. They wanted to make sure I would butt out. and let the poor witch victims finally rest in peace."

"Or else, huh? Tough guys."

"Well, I understand their concern. They're well motivated. I told them that as far as I'm concerned it's probably best to let them be. The skeletons are a significant historical find but if moved or exhibited, they just would have been further exploited, poor souls."

They sat quietly a moment.

"But now nobody will ever know what a gallant, courageous person Philip English was to provide a proper burial for the witch victims," said Joe.

"Well, he didn't want any fanfare anyway, it seems. I guess he was a nice, quiet guy like you."

Then Helen moved in close to Joe. "Hold me," she said. "I'm freezing."

He held her close. "I love this boat, Helen," he said, "smell and all but I'm really looking forward to sharing a Stone Harbor apartment with you."

She looked at him closely, patted his hand, and let out a little sigh. "Gee, Joe, after the fright Mabel suffered over the Mary Rose coffee thing, I think I'd better stay with her for a while 'til she calms down."

There was a long silence. The *Working Girl* rocked and creaked. Joe coughed and then smiled.

"Okay," he said, "I guess I'll just have to move in here aboard the *Working Girl.*"

Helen smiled back. "Well, then, you'll have to start paying me rent for keeping you warm."

THE END
Salem's Secret

Salem, Massachusetts
1692-1999

Other titles available from
Old Saltbox Publishing House

OLD NEW ENGLAND SERIES

Number 1A.............Strange Superstitions

Number 2A.............Curious Customs and Cures

Number 3A.............Sugar & Spice and Everything ...

Number 3B.............Christmas Memories

Number 4A.............Haunted Happenings

Number 5A.............Ancient Mysteries

Number 6A.............Cruel and Unusual Punishments

Number 7A.............Lighthouse Mysteries of the North Atlantic

Number 8A.............Haunted Ships of the North Atlantic

Chandler - Smith — COLLECTIBLE CLASSICS SERIES

Number 1................New England's Witches And Wizards

Number 2................New England's Ghostly Haunts

Number 3................New England's Marvelous Monsters

Number 4................New England's Mad And Mysterious Men

Number 5................New England's Strange Sea Sagas

Number 6................Finding New England's Shipwrecks And Treasures

Number 7................New England's War Wonders

Number 8................New England's Visitors From Outer Space

Number 9................The Horrors of Salem's Witch Dungeon

Number 10.............The Old Irish Of New England

Number 11.............New England's Naughty Navy

Number 12.............New England's Viking And Indian Wars

Number 13.............New England's Riotous Revolution

Number 14.............New England's Pirates And Lost Treasures

Number 15.............New England's Mountain Madness

Number 16.............New England's Things That Go Bump In The Night